Muffin Ventured, Muffin Gained

Baker's Rise Mysteries

Book Four

R. A. Hutchins

The characters, locations and events portrayed in this story are wholly the product of the author's imagination. Any similarity to any persons, whether living or dead, is purely coincidental.

Cover Design by Molly Burton at cozycoverdesigns.com

Muffin recipe kindly created by Emma Carlton at Sweet Patisserie, 168 Park View, Whitley Bay, UK

ISBN: 9798404972207

For my beautiful Belle,
You are my sunshine! xxx

CONTENTS

If you follow this list in order, you will have made a perfect batch of ***Maraschino Cherry, Lemon & Almond Muffins*** *to enjoy while you read!*

ONE

Flora's smile was wide and her heart happy as she surveyed her little bookshop with pleasure. Decorated in pastel greens and yellows, in a more subtle take on Reggie's own feathered colour palette, the tones were offset by the wooden units and shelving. A small leather sofa sat in one corner – A gift from Harry, as he said he had no use for it now he was living with his wife, Betty – and in the opposite space a small children's bookshelf in the shape of a train sat beside a tiny table and chairs, perfectly proportioned for little people.

"It looks lovely," Amy said, coming up behind her.

"Looks lovely," Reggie parroted back, chirping happily on Flora's shoulder. His ability to pick up on her emotions had only increased in the time they had spent together, and he now basked in the shared glow of their success. The shelves which lined the walls held a wide selection of books – the suggestions of the villagers had been included, as well as classics, local history, children's books, and quite a few that had been bought on Amy's recommendation. The young woman had a voracious reading habit, and her literary knowledge had helped Flora a great deal in planning which books to offer up front. Flora knew that she had probably overspent – rather substantially – on the initial purchase of stock for the place. Adam had cautioned her to invest only a little and then purchase more books as and when profits from the shop allowed, but as with most things, Flora had become carried away with her new venture and had spent money which should have probably been invested in the renovations up at the big house. 'In for a penny, in for a pound,' and all that. To justify this decision to herself, Flora had decided to postpone the house clearance company who were meant to clear the bedrooms in January, and they were now coming in a month's time, at the beginning of March. To be honest, Flora hadn't ventured up to The Rise very much since Billy's death, as the memories were still too raw. In the spring, she had told herself, there would be new beginnings all round. Hopefully by then, there might be sign of the money coming from her ex-husband,

Gregory, for Flora's share in their town house. Their former marital home had been put on the market in the hope the sale would cover some of his debts while the man himself was answering police questions over fraud and deception.

"Aw, it is beautiful, you have done a great job," Tanya said, coming through from the tearoom, where the tinkle of the bell over the door told Flora that the last customers of the day were just leaving, "all set for the grand opening this weekend."

Her words brought Flora back to the present, "Yes, I think that's everything!" Flora cast her eyes around the room for a final time, reaching up to touch the crocheted bunting, so delicate it was almost like lace, which Jean and Sally had made with the village Knit and Natter group. From next week, the group would be held here, in the Bookshop on the Rise, and Flora couldn't wait to see her little space come to life. For the moment though, she had the big opening to get through, and the first public reading of the initial book in her series of Reggie's adventures. A grey thought clouded Flora's happiness for a moment.

"A penny for them," Amy said in her quiet way.

"You look suddenly distracted," Tanya added, when Flora didn't reply.

"My Flora," Reggie chirped, nuzzling against her neck.

"What? Oh sorry! I was just thinking about the grand opening on Saturday. I have four more days to organise someone to cut the ribbon for us. I had put all my hopes on Clarissa Cutter coming to do the honours, and her personal assistant did seem hopeful when I spoke to him last week, but I haven't heard anything since, despite leaving a voicemail and sending two emails."

"Never heard of her," Tanya said tutting, " I still say you should cut the ribbon yourself, Flora, you have done all the hard work, written the stories, you deserve to do it."

"Thank you, but she's very famous in the local art scene as an illustrator, and I desperately want her to agree to doing the artwork for my books. Even if I don't get a publisher, I could go ahead and publish them myself if they were professionally illustrated. She is apparently very picky about which clients she takes on though, so I hoped I could butter her up with this opening ceremony gig."

"Well, I am sure there are others who could help with the books," Tanya said bluntly.

"My Gareth might know someone," Amy spoke up

timidly, "his wife – his late wife – was an artist, there are beautiful landscapes of hers which he still has on display. Perhaps he knows one of her friends from the art world who could help?" Amy wrapped her arms around her waist as if embarrassed by having said so much at once. Her straight blonde hair was scraped back into a high ponytail, emphasising her huge eyes and shy smile, and both of the older women smiled back encouragingly. Flora, in particular, was so happy to see her friend come out of her shell a bit in recent weeks as they'd worked together selecting books and deciding how to arrange the shelves.

"Such a tragedy, that was," Tanya said sadly.

"I'm sorry, I knew he had little Lewis, but I didn't realise his wife had passed," Flora admitted, realising that she hadn't thought about it at all, in fact, other than being used to seeing Gareth and Lewis around the village together.

"Yes, Lewis will be four next month and starts school in September," Amy said, "he attends a nursery in Alnwick a few days a week and the other days he spends with Gareth's mum and dad while he's at work."

"Died in childbirth," Tanya chimed in, "so awful. Though I have only heard the story, I wasn't yet in the village then."

"It really was," Amy's face clouded as she remembered, "I was a friend of them both, you see, though they were a few years older than me. I met Natalie at a book club. She was such an avid reader and such a talented artist. It took Gareth and I until eighteen months ago to admit we had feelings for each other, it felt like we were dishonouring her memory to speak it out loud, somehow," Amy blushed a delicate pink and fussed with the shelf nearest to her.

"You are such a good match," Tanya linked arms with the younger woman, "and I'm sure Nat would have wanted Gareth to be happy. I have only heard lovely things about the woman."

"Yes, and we've taken it slowly, I'm still living in the village with my mam and dad," Amy added, as if justifying it to herself.

"Well, if you wouldn't mind asking Gareth," Flora said, hopefully, "if it wouldn't be too awkward, then I'd be very grateful. The clock is ticking and with every day that passes I have less hope that the esteemed Ms. Cutter will grace us with her presence."

"All the more reason to find someone else," Tanya said, nodding her head decisively, "anyway I'd better be getting back to my Pat, see you in the morning."

"Thanks Tanya," Flora ran her hands down her floral apron. She wanted to clear up in the tearoom quickly as Adam was coming round for supper.

"Flora?" Amy stopped her as she was about to walk through the opening between the two shops.

"Yes?"

"Thank you so much for letting me help, you don't know how happy I've been this past month. I mean, I enjoy hairdressing an' all, and it was such luck that Linda decided to close the salon in January to go and visit her sick father, but I would love to be here more… more permanently."

"Ah Amy, I would love that too, but at the moment, I can't afford to take on anyone else. What with paying Tanya to help in the tearoom I daren't take on any more outgoings at the moment."

"Of course, of course," Amy was blushing deeply and wringing her hands, "just keep me in mind, if…"

"You'd always be my first choice!" Flora patted Amy's arm and the younger woman went to fetch her hoodie from the antique coat stand which Adam had carried down from the big house for Flora, and which now stood proudly in the corner.

"First choice! She's a corker!" Reggie parroted as they waved Amy goodbye. Flora did feel a certain amount of guilt and dismay that she was unable to offer Amy even a part-time position, especially after all the help she had given and time she had spent voluntarily up at the bookshop. Sighing gently, Flora locked the door, turned the sign to closed and went to clear up the few dishes that were left. Who knew what the next few months would bring? If the bookshop took off and Flora was able to publish her books, then perhaps she would be able to afford to hire Amy after all.

Yet, behind it all the shadow of The Rise loomed over her. Some days Flora thought that perhaps if she had just inherited the coach house and stable buildings which had become the tearoom and bookshop, then life would be much easier. The manor house seemed to be a poisoned chalice somehow. Flora knew that she would need to make some decisions about where to invest her time and resources in the future – a decision for another day, though. For now, she would enjoy the progress they had made in this first month of the year.

TWO

Flora had just changed into a pretty floral jumper and cord trousers, having showered when she got home to the coach house from the tearoom, when she heard Adam's car pull up outside.

"Visitors! Visitors with money!" Reggie shrieked as Flora hurried up the small hallway, hearing Adam's footsteps crunching on the gravel path outside.

"Shush, silly bird," Flora chastised gently.

"You silly bird!" Reggie parried back, just as Flora opened the front door.

"Ah, as complimentary as always," Adam joked, smirking as he hurried in out of the cold.

"Yes, well," Flora blushed as Adam bent down to kiss

her sweetly on the lips.

"Brought you some red, thought you might need something to calm the nerves now it's less than a week till the grand opening," Adam handed Flora a bag with a bottle-shaped bulge.

"Thank you, that's exactly what I need," Flora replied gratefully.

"Phil didn't turn up again today did he?" Adam's voice and expression hardened for a second before he quickly returned to his usual good humour.

"No, no, thankfully not."

"Well, make sure to give him short shrift if he does."

Flora knew that Adam was only reacting to the many times she had moaned about Phil popping up – both at the bookshop and her home – over the past month. Always with a suggestion for a book she should stock, or some other excuse, Flora had begun to dread his unexpected arrivals. Phil, on the other hand, seemed to have the thick skin of a rhinoceros, for he never reacted to either her subtle hints or Flora's increasingly overt declarations that she was busy and had all the help she needed.

"I still have no idea what his ulterior motive is," Flora

admitted, "but the whole thing is certainly draining."

"Well, why don't you just ask him outright? What's the harm? Take the bull by the horns so to speak."

Flora mulled this over as she filled the kettle and added some instant coffee granules to a mug for Adam, whilst he poured her a glass of wine. Their actions were easy and synchronised now, so often had they been in this same space doing exactly the same thing.

Coming to put her arms around his waist, Flora whispered, "I might just do that, but let's not give him any more headspace right now, tell me about your day."

"It's been a strange one, to be sure," Adam said, once they were settled on the sofa in the small sitting room together, "can't give you any details, as you know, what with confidentiality and all that, but I've spent the day over Alnwick way beginning an investigation into the death of an artist."

"Not Lizzie, the pet portrait painter?" Flora panicked for her friend, "She's meant to be coming over tomorrow with Reggie's picture to hang in the book shop. I asked her to hold onto it for me until the room was all ready to display it."

"No, lass, no, it was a bloke. Older gentleman, some kind of critic I think, by the newspaper cuttings he had pinned up in his studio."

"Oh, that's okay then, well, I mean it's not, it's awful, but," Flora stuttered and stumbled over her words.

"Don't worry, I know what you meant. Poor guy took a tumble down some stairs, but the injury to his head suggests foul play."

Visions of poor Ray Dodds, smacked in the head with one of his own frozen pies by his own estranged daughter, who had then tumbled to his death, came to Flora's mind and she shuddered involuntarily.

"Aw, I shouldn't have mentioned it, sorry," Adam pulled Flora into his side gently and held her close, "just been a strange day, that's all. That area of the countryside, outside the main town, is normally crime free. The local coppers spend more time looking for stray cats and catching speeding cars than anything else!"

"No, don't apologise, I want to hear about your day. Thinking of artists, though, I'd better try phoning that illustrator one more time."

"Has she still not got back to you?"

"No, it's been radio silence since I spoke to her P.A. over a week ago. That man sounded lovely, and I've no doubt he's got his work cut out for him trying to deal with her, she's a bit of an ogre by all accounts."

"Well then why bother with her?"

"You do have a point, Tanya said exactly the same thing," Flora mulled it over, then came to a decision, "I'll try once more then draw a line under it."

"Okay love, I'll just pop the television on while you do that," Adam squeezed Flora's hand as she stood to make the phone call.

Doubting her own decision, now that she was standing in the chilly kitchen listening to the phone ring unanswered on the other end of the line, Flora was almost shocked when finally an annoyed voice sounded in her ear.

"Hello?"

"Oh, hello!"

"Who is this?"

"It's Flora, Flora Miller, from Baker's Rise, I…"

"Never heard of you!"

"Oh, well, I spoke to Martin Loughbrough, your personal assistant…"

"I know fine well who he is!"

Flora took a deep breath, "it's about cutting the ribbon at my bookshop opening," she decided not to mention her children's books until after they had been acquainted in person.

"I don't do just any old event, you know!"

"Well, I, it's just that the local press are coming, maybe even the Newcastle Chronicle and I wanted…" Flora was interrupted yet again, which was just as well, as she hadn't actually heard anything back from the newspaper in question.

"The Chronicle you say? Well, why didn't you mention that first? I charge two hundred pounds for in person events. I'll get Martin to phone you for the details, then he'll come along the day before to make sure everything meets my requirements."

"Your requirements? Well, I…." but the other woman had already hung up, "How rude!" Flora spoke aloud to Reggie who had flown into the room, no doubt hearing her rising exasperation.

"Rude! Rude!" he echoed back to her.

"I take it you got through then?" Adam asked, coming into the kitchen to join them.

"I did, and well, let's just say I think her reputation is very well deserved! And she wants to charge me two hundred pounds for the pleasure of being insulted by her!"

"That's ridiculous! For cutting a piece of ribbon? I'll do it for you for half as much," Adam winked at her, then his tone became serious once again, "call her back and cancel then, love."

He had a point, but Flora felt that she'd persevered for too long to back out now. This woman, as odious as she seemed, could mean make or break for the Reggie stories, so Flora decided to go ahead with the booking. After all, she would only have to put up with the artist for an hour or so, what harm could it do?

THREE

Tuesday brought with it clear skies and a milder temperature, lifting Flora's mood and making the short walk to the tearoom a pleasure for the first time in many days. Reggie flew above her, squawking happily as if he too felt the sudden freedom from the murky days of January, which had seemed to all blend into one long month of dank darkness.

The daily delivery from George Jones was in its plastic box at the side of the building as per usual, though Flora was producing more of her own baked goods these days. She often had scones fresh from the tearoom oven, ready to serve at opening time, as well as pies and fruit cake which she made a couple of times a week. Flora hoped that George's nose wouldn't be put out of joint when he realised that she had used a new provider for the refreshments at the bookshop's opening event. An impulsive trip to the coast, arranged by Adam to try to lift her spirits a couple of weeks ago, had led Flora to discover a patisserie in the seaside town of Whitley Bay. Finding she shared a lot in common with the owner, Flora had invited her to create a new recipe for the grand opening. So, there would be sweet muffins and hot drinks, with some fairy cakes for the children which Betty was making, and carrot cake courtesy of Lily up at the farm. Nothing ordered from George, which did make Flora feel slightly guilty, but she shrugged off the feeling as she put on a fresh apron and turned on the huge coffee machine.

Reggie was just dozing off on his perch when the bell above the door tinkled and Lizzie popped her head around.

"Hello Flora! I've got your painting in the car, if you could just hold this door open for me so I can bring it in."

"Of course," Flora rushed to grab the door, a spark of excitement flaring inside her, as Lizzie ducked back out. What with losing Billy and then attending his funeral, Gregory turning up alive, and then the Christmas festivities and talent show, not to mention getting the bookshop set up, Flora hadn't been up to

Alnwick to see the finished painting. She couldn't wait to see the portrait of Reggie, literally larger than life, and taking pride of place in her new shop.

"Wow, Flora, this place is as pretty as a picture," Lizzie exclaimed as they went straight through to the bookshop, the large, framed picture held between them.

"Thank you, it has certainly been a labour of love, but I'm thrilled with how it's all turned out," Flora blushed slightly and indicated with her spare hand the space which was to house Reggie's portrait.

"Ta da!" Lizzie removed the covering sheet with a flourish.

"Oh Lizzie, it's perfect!" Flora ran her finger down the gilt frame as she admired the painted parrot in all his splendour, "You've captured his little – or should I say big – personality perfectly!"

"I'm so glad you like it, Flora, it's such a relief when a client is happy with the finished product!"

"Ooh sexy beast!" Reggie declared, landing on Flora's shoulder and admiring the picture of himself.

"I guess Reggie is pleased with it too!" Lizzie chuckled.

"Yes, he's certainly not the shy and retiring type," Flora laughed, "I hope you received your invitation in the post, Lizzie, I'm sure everyone will be keen to meet the artist of this fine piece."

"Thank you, Flora, yes, I'm very much looking forward to your grand opening."

"Well, you won't be the only artist in attendance, actually," Flora added, as they made their way back into the tearoom for a cuppa, "I've got a lady coming to cut the ribbon. Truth be told, I'm kind of regretting it now, but I had been hoping she would agree to illustrate my Reggie books."

"Oh? I know most of the other artists in the area, who is it?"

"Clarissa Cutter," Flora paused as she saw the expression on Lizzie's normally-cheerful face change, and the air could suddenly be cut with a knife, "I take it you know of her?"

"Not just of her, unfortunately, I know the woman herself," Lizzie sat down at the nearest table as if the air had been taken out of her sails, "we were at college together, many, many moons ago. She was just the same then, critical and judgemental. Let's just say she's always been my loudest critic even since we graduated

– doesn't see pet portraits as proper art, you see."

"Oh, I'm so sorry, Lizzie, I had no idea."

"Well, she's lost me some big clients in the past, local landowners and the like, but it's all water under the bridge now."

"You will still come, won't you?" Flora was beginning to wish she'd never done the internet search which had led her to the infamous Ms. Cutter in the first place.

"I… yes, of course," though Lizzie said it on a quiet sigh and Flora got the impression that the other woman would only attend now out of a sense of obligation.

The day passed slowly, giving Flora far too much time to think. Tanya was not starting her new schedule in the tearoom until the following week, when the bookshop was open, so Flora pottered around in the too-quiet room, rearranging crockery and dusting shelves, then moving into the bookshop and clearing a spot to house her vintage typewriter, which she was planning on bringing over from the coach house as a bit of a talking point. Then she turned her attention to writing out a small notice explaining how the library corner would work. There wasn't much to explain really, as it was a trust system based on the borrower signing a book out in the notebook provided and then crossing it off the list once it was returned. At the moment, there were only four shelves dedicated to the little library, with books donated from locals and from Flora's own collection, but Flora hoped this would grow quickly.

Just as she was wondering if it would be worth cutting her losses for the day, as even Reggie seemed to be bored and had taken to flying loops of the room on repeat, the bell rang and Betty bustled in with Jean close behind her.

"Flora lass, get that kettle on, I'm fair parched!" Betty spoke across the room before she was even fully inside. Reggie paused his flying and landed on the table next to the door, as if taking up sentry position when he saw little Tina the terrier in Betty's arms.

Flora smiled, happy to have some company, and especially that of two of her favourite neighbours, "Of course, ladies, take a seat and I'll be right with you. A pot of Earl Grey coming up!"

"Aye, and we'll share one of those scones you make so nicely now," Betty added, causing Flora's face to heat under the praise.

"Have you been busy?" Flora asked, when all three were sat with steaming cups of tea.

"Well, it was the monthly Women's Institute lunch today, and things got rather heated," Jean said, raising a quick eyebrow in Betty's direction.

"Oh? I thought you were all having a meal at the pub, I think I recall Shona mentioning it," Flora said.

"Aye well, the food was beautiful, young Shona knows how to lay on a good spread, it was the company that was questionable," Betty tut-tutted, and Flora knew better than to interrupt. She and Jean sat quietly, waiting for the tirade which was sure to follow, "That Edwina Edwards thinks she knows everything about everything now she's in charge, she forgets that I ran the W.I. for fifteen years myself!" Betty's voice rose in agitation.

"Oh, I'm sure she knows that, you do remind her often enough!" Jean winked at Flora as she spoke.

"Aye well, what does she mean by wanting to change everything? We've always met at the church hall every Thursday at seven, now she wants to make it Friday at eight. What is she thinking?" Betty spoke long and passionately until even Reggie had clearly heard enough.

"Time for bed! Time for bed!" he chimed in, taking advantage of one of the few moments when Betty paused for breath.

"Um, not quite," Flora tapped his beak as he came to rest on her arm, whilst Jean smothered her chuckle behind her hand.

"Anyway," Betty scowled at the bird, "I'd better be getting back to make Harry's tea."

"Well, don't forget about the bookshop opening on Saturday, it wouldn't be the same without you there," Flora tried to pour oil on troubled waters.

Betty huffed, as if bringing an end to her former subject of conversation, then rubbed Flora's arm and smiled, "Aye lass, I'll have those little cakes ready for the young'uns and be here prompt with Harry."

"Are you sure you don't need any help with the setting up?" Jean asked kindly.

"I think I'll be okay, I've got Tanya and Amy roped in to help me, and Adam of course."

The two women said their goodbyes and Flora released a small sigh of relief to be locking the door and turning the sign to closed.

"A soak in the bath and a final read-through of the story I'm going to present on Saturday are in order now, Reggie," Flora declared as her feathered friend settled on her shoulder, "but first, washing up!"

FOUR

The church hall felt positively arctic on Wednesday evening as a small group gathered for Jazzercise. The numbers were up from normal, as there had been an influx of people who had taken on a keep fit regime as part of their New Year's resolutions. Flora shook her arms and legs to keep warm, and when that didn't work took to jumping on the spot.

"Sorry about the heating, or rather lack of it, the old boiler has finally given up the ghost, I think," Sally's teeth chattered as she spoke, "James is speaking to the Bishop tomorrow about getting the funds for a new one."

"Well, at least it gives us the impetus to keep moving!" Flora joked, though secretly she wished she was cosy at home with Reggie. She smoothed down her long t-shirt, which almost reached her knees over her leggings, feeling self-conscious about the new curves over her hips and stomach which she'd developed since opening the tearoom. Flora made a mental note to book an appointment with the practice nurse to talk about her hormone levels, as surely this development must be due to her age, and could have nothing to do with the cakes and pastries she so loved!

Tanya was doing an elaborate series of warm up moves at the front of the hall, decked out in a pink neon vest top, yellow neon tiny shorts and green neon leg warmers. She was like a traffic light that had got stuck in the eighties! Flora suppressed a smile as she saw Tanya casting a suspicious glance at two men who had just arrived. Ordinarily, this Jazzercise class attracted only a group of local women, though Flora knew from her life in London that most exercise classes nowadays were open to anyone. It was only in this remote part of the country that people seemed to stick to the stereotypes. Tanya made no comment to the newcomers, however, simply kept contorting herself into positions which would have Flora laid up for the next few days if she even so much as tried them.

Just as Tanya was set to press play on the music, the doors opened with a rush of icy air and Amy hurried inside. Her eyes were red and blotchy, and not just from the cold, Flora thought. Sally clearly shared her view as she silently took Amy by the arm and steered her straight through to the kitchen at the side of the hall. Keen to postpone the actual exercise for as long as possible, whilst also being worried for her friend of course, Flora hurried after them.

"Amy, are you okay? Did you walk here?" Sally asked quietly once they had shut the door to give them some privacy. Flora turned on the gas burners on the large hob to blast the air with a bit of heat, as they were all shivering uncontrollably now.

"No, Gareth and Lewis dropped me off," Amy's bottom lip quivered and tears started falling anew.

"Are they both okay? Has something happened?" Sally's gentle tone was calming and Flora simply rubbed Amy's arm and let the vicar's wife do the talking.

"They're fine. Sorry, I'm being pathetic."

"No, no you're not, not at all. We just don't like to see you upset. Perhaps there's something we can do to help?"

"If Gareth and I had had an argument or something,

then it would be easier to explain. I'm being silly, really, it's just that I mentioned when I was getting out of the car that we'd have to meet up one evening and go through the finances to see if we have enough to get a place together – he doesn't want me to move into the house he shared with Natalie, and I understand that – and he went all cold on me, and just said, 'Bye then.' I mean, I don't know what to think. I don't want to replace his wife, but I love him, I…" Amy began to sway on her feet and Flora noticed just in time to catch the younger woman as her knees buckled and she fell backwards. Sally rushed forwards and the two women laid Amy on the cold linoleum floor.

"Do you think we should get Doctor Edwards?" Flora asked.

"No, I think she's just fainted," Sally rubbed Amy's cheek gently with the back of her hand and the young woman came round again.

"What..?"

"You just fainted, nothing a good cup of sweet tea won't sort out," Sally said, "no, don't try to get up yet, wait a moment. I bet the room's still spinning isn't it? I fainted a lot in my last pregnancy, with Megan, and I learnt not to jump up again too quickly or I'd be back down in a flash!" She was rewarded with a weak smile from Amy.

Flora tried to hide her concern behind a cheerful façade, secretly very grateful that Sally had been there, "I'll put the kettle on, shall I?"

"Why don't you both come across to the vicarage? It's warmer in there and the girls are in bed."

"Will the vicar not mind?" Amy whispered, "I hate to be a bother."

"Not at all, he'll be in his study most likely, he says the sermon writing flows better in the evenings."

Flora and Sally helped Amy up and propped her against the counter top with Sally's arm around her waist. Flora turned off the hob burners and rushed through to tell Tanya what had happened. Her friend's eyebrows shot up farther than Flora could have imagined was natural, and Flora knew that Tanya would like nothing better than to postpone the class and come to the vicarage with them but, ever the professional, she barely even missed a beat, even taking the excuse of the pause to tell the men that they needed to be putting in one hundred and ten percent effort to her class! Flora smiled and hurried back, helping Sally to guide Amy to the vicarage.

Once they were all settled in front of the fire in the large sitting room – which Flora noted had been redecorated in a cheery lemon since her last fateful visit to the house, when Sally and James' predecessors were still in residence – Sally asked Amy if she was feeling better now.

"Yes, much, thank you," Amy replied, setting her cup of hot, sweet tea down on the mahogany side table, "I don't know what came over me, but I haven't eaten since this morning so that was probably it. I was looking after Lewis while Gareth was at work, as his mum is ill today, and I should've made something for myself when I gave him his lunch."

"You should bring him round to play with Megan sometime," Sally suggested," I think they're both starting Reception class together in the Autumn, and she'd love to show him the toys she received for Christmas!"

"Did you have no evening meal?" Flora asked, changing the subject completely, but almost shocked that someone could go so long without their body telling them they needed to eat – even though she had done the same thing many times when she worked in the City.

"No, Gareth got home later than expected, and I didn't

want to miss Jazzercise," Amy blushed.

"Well, let me get you a sandwich," Sally had jumped up and crossed the room before Amy could protest, leaving Flora alone with the younger woman.

"Perhaps you could call Gareth," Flora suggested tentatively, the crackle of the open fire the only other sound in the room.

"He'll probably be bathing Lewis by now, they were going to get fish and chips on the way home, I don't like to intrude."

"I'm sure he wouldn't see it as intruding, especially if he knew you were upset," Flora thought back to the many times she had called Adam in floods of tears.

"Yes, you're right, I'll call him when I get home," Amy smiled, but it didn't reach her eyes and Flora could see that it was forced. Knowing how shy Amy was, Flora wondered how many friends the younger woman had to confide in.

"Why don't you call into the bookshop tomorrow, or Friday, and we can have a natter?" Flora suggested. Not that she had a great track record with relationships., she knew, though she hoped Adam may be the one to change that. But she also knew that talking things over helped, if there was one thing she'd learned since coming to the village it was that. Perhaps now it was her turn to lend the proverbial shoulder to cry on.

"I will do, Flora, thank you," Amy tried to surreptitiously wipe her eyes as Sally re-joined them with a plate full of sandwiches and three side plates.

"Perks of living in a vicarage," she joked, "we're always prepared for visitors!"

As Flora made her way down the path past the duck pond half an hour later, her phone pinged with a message from Adam wondering if she'd like a quick drink in the Bun in the Oven after her exercise class. It had been sent over half an hour ago, but there must have been no reception at the vicarage. The phone signal in this area was so hit and miss, Flora was glad she didn't have to rely on it. Thankfully, at her elevated position on the hill of The Rise, she rarely encountered the problem.

Adam had just come off duty, but was keen to see her. Flora smiled to herself as she typed back. The Flora of old would have worried that her hair was scraped back in a bun, she was wearing a t-shirt big enough for a giant and the overall look was far from flattering. This Flora, however, cared only that she would spend some time with the man she loved, and not a jot that the villagers might get an eyeful of her in her workout gear. With a spring in her step, she headed down to the local pub, thankful for the life she had found here. Now that the deaths and investigations of last year had been laid to rest, and the New Year had brought with it hope and possibility, Flora was sure that they had all turned a corner and could move forward free of ghosts from the past.

FIVE

Reggie basked in the glow of all the attention which he received on Friday morning, with first Shona popping by for a chat and then Betty. He even gave a cordial "Welcome to the tearoom" to little Tina when Betty sat with her on her lap and, much to Flora's amazement and relief, refrained from making any rude comments when the third visitor to the café that day turned out to be Phil.

"Phil, what a… surprise," Flora stumbled between saying what was polite and what she actually felt, which was to wonder why the man had turned up yet again. It was a school day, so he surely couldn't have come in for a leisurely cuppa, "Shouldn't you be in school?" It sounded too blunt even to Flora's ears, and Reggie clearly picked up on the new terseness in her voice, adding his own, "Not that jerk!" for good measure. *Knew it was too good to last*, Flora thought to herself, as she tapped Reggie's beak gently to dissuade any further outburst.

"Ah yes, lunch break," Phil blushed a deep shade of red.

Before he could say anything else, however, Flora rushed ahead with, "Goodness, is it that time already? I have an appointment at one o'clock!" That much was true, as Clarissa Cutter's assistant, Martin, was due to call in to finalise the details for the following day.

"Oh, well I won't keep you then, I just wanted to see if there was anything else I could do to help with the books?"

Flora cast her arm in the direction of the bookshop, which could be seen through the open doorway in the adjoining wall behind them, "As you can see, we're all set up and ready to go!"

"Excellent," though Phil didn't sound quite happy about the fact, nor did his face reflect any pleasure whatsoever.

Deciding that enough was enough, Flora offered the man a seat at the nearest table, "Phil, whilst I have been grateful for your advice about book choices and your repeated offers of help, I wonder if there isn't something… something prompting them?" Flora sat back to study Phil's face, which was even redder now. Flora hoped to goodness that the cause wasn't something of an amorous nature. As the silence between them lengthened and became thoroughly uncomfortable, with Reggie flying circles above their heads in a pointless repetition which seemed to reflect the futility of their own discussion, Flora cleared her throat to speak again.

Before she could say a word, however, Phil spoke quickly, as if he were forcing the words out, "I'm sorry, Flora, I didn't mean to, I mean I did want to help, but I hadn't intended it to make you uncomfortable. I just hoped that… well, I've written a book you see!"

To say she was surprised was an understatement, "Well, why didn't you just say so, Phil? You know I have been doing the very same thing."

"Yes, ah, well not quite the same, as yours is children's fiction, very wholesome, and mine is… well, it's historical, but ah, more of the adult persuasion. More for the, ah, discerning reader, if you know what I mean."

"Oh!" Flora didn't know what to say, and wasn't sure she wanted to know what he meant, as she felt her own face reddening under Phil's implication. She didn't consider herself a prude by any means, but she certainly didn't want to be thinking of any kind of romance or liaisons where Phil was concerned, whether simply the product of his imagination or not.

"And I was hoping, once I've self-published it in a couple of months, that you might consider stocking it in the Bookshop on the Rise?" Phil rushed on, his tone hopeful, "Helping out another local author and all that."

Flora took a big gulp of air, and silently wished for once that Reggie would make one of his unsuitable interruptions. As it was, the silly bird was now sitting lazily on his perch, apparently having exhausted himself by acting like a polite parrot earlier in the morning. No, it was all up to her to think of something to say.

"Well, Phil, it's not that I don't think there's a place for every type of literature, it's just that I'm not sure that place is in my bookshop, if you know what I mean?" Flora was met with stony silence as Phil mopped his brow with a grubby grey handkerchief he must've produced from his pocket, so she ploughed on, "Imagine Betty Bentley or one of the other ladies from the W.I. stumbling across it when they're looking for an Agatha Christie or Jane Austen."

"Pah! I'm sure these villagers have a lot of carnal secrets you couldn't even guess at! Old Harold had the right idea, he knew none of them were whiter than white like they claim to be!"

At the mention of her predecessor at The Rise and his sordid collection of personal files on the villagers, the conversation had taken one step too far for Flora's liking, "Well, if that was all, Phil?"

"So, you won't even consider it? You could read it first…"

The old Flora, people pleaser extraordinaire, would have said yes just to appease the man. The new Flora, however, simply shook her head firmly, "there's no need, Phil, I'm afraid it isn't the kind of book I'm hoping to sell. I think you'll probably have more luck on the internet."

"I had thought you different, Flora, when you first arrived. Like a breath of fresh air, in fact, and now I see you're just as stuffy as all the rest!" With that Phil stomped out, slamming the door behind him and causing the bell above to tinkle uncontrollably for a few seconds.

"Stupid git!" Reggie screeched after him, whilst Flora simply sat, somewhat astounded.

In fact, Flora didn't even hear the bell above the door go a few minutes later – it was Reggie who alerted her to the new arrival, "Visitors! Visitors with money!" he squawked as a very well presented gentleman entered. Looking to be in his early fifties, and particularly well groomed, wearing a three piece suit complete with pocket watch and silk cravat, the man spoke with a soft, melodious voice that was in total keeping with his demeanour.

"Mrs. Miller, I presume?"

"Hm? Oh yes, Flora please, you must be Martin Loughbrough."

"Indeed," he smiled brightly, and Flora stood to take the offered hand where Martin had removed his smart leather glove.

"My apologies," Flora began, "I was in my own little world there."

"Not at all, dear, I imagine you must appreciate the peace when it comes in a lovely tearoom like this."

Flora beamed under the praise and even Reggie, who had come to sit on her shoulder, puffed out his little chest with pride.

"Please do take a seat and I'll make us a pot of tea," Flora said, directing the man to the table nearest the counter, where they could still talk whilst she prepared the drinks.

"And who is this little chap?" Martin asked, reaching out a hand to stroke Reggie. For once, the parrot didn't choose to either shy away or rush headlong to greet the stranger. He stood very still, as if assessing the situation, before chirping "My Flora!" rather possessively.

"Reggie!" Flora blushed and popped the bird back onto his perch, "Mr. Loughbrough has come to discuss the grand opening tomorrow."

"Quite so, quite so," Martin said, as he delicately removed his other glove, and then his overcoat and hat, placing them gently on the coat stand which he had spotted just over the threshold in the bookshop, "Ms. Cutter has, what you might call, a rigorous set of pre-event checks and requirements."

"Oh?" Flora tried to hide her rising concern as she bustled about in the kitchen area. There wasn't much time to be getting things in now if she wasn't prepared enough for her guest of honour, "And what kind of ..?"

"Shall we discuss it over this lovely tea you've made? Earl Grey? My favourite, and such beautiful china cups too," in just a few seconds, Martin had put Flora back at ease, and she could tell why someone with the reputation of Clarissa Cutter, for being a bit of a diva, needed someone like him to smooth the way. Sitting down opposite the man, and running her fingers over the creases in her apron, Flora prepared herself for what Mr. Loughbrough had to say.

SIX

"Her own bathroom?" Flora realised her voice had become high pitched and rather incredulous, but after the list of demands she'd already heard – which included a specific brand of Northumberland spring water, a box of tissues made from recycled paper and laced with lavender oil, organic hand cream and unhindered access to any members of the local press to give uninterrupted interviews before anyone else – this about took the biscuit!

"I'm afraid so. She has had some, ah, rather distasteful experiences in the past when it comes to unhygienic conveniences."

"Well my convenience… is very convenient! And hygienic!" Flora blurted, "Besides there is only the one here, that serves both the tearoom and bookshop."

"Ah, is there really nowhere else? I spotted a big manor house on the hill, that is definitely more to Ms. Cutter's taste."

"The Rise? No, that's all closed up for now. Besides, all the bathrooms need replacing, I've only just had new plumbing put in," Flora knew she was rambling. With a sinking feeling, she realised there was only one option, "My own home, in the converted coach house, is only a few minutes along the footpath. Ms. Cutter would be welcome to use the facilities if she has need."

"Perfect, thank you, she will stop there on arrival to make sure she is looking presentable and to do her pre-public appearance vocal warm ups."

"Oh, well I won't be home, then, I'll be here, waiting for her with everyone else."

"Is there anyone else who could..?"

Flora racked her brain to think of someone who wouldn't rub the artist up the wrong way, then felt guilty for thinking of her friends so negatively, "Amy, yes Amy," Flora couldn't hide the relief in her voice, "a lovely young woman, knows a lot about books."

"Perfect," Martin himself seemed relieved that they had found a solution. Flora didn't envy him the job of having to tell his boss her demands hadn't been met, so no doubt he was happy that wasn't the case this time, "that is everything, I think. Oh, just don't wear blue."

"Blue? Whyever not?"

"It is Ms. Cutter's colour of choice for press photographs, and she doesn't like anyone else to be in the same hue."

"Well, really," Flora bit her tongue so hard it hurt her not to speak, but she had come so far in securing this woman to cut the ribbon, it would be silly to fail now, "Ah, Mr. Loughbrough, one last thing…"

"Of course, my dear."

"Do you happen to know if Clarissa has any openings in her schedule – her schedule of illustrative work that is – for this coming year?"

Martin appeared to blanch and for the first time his suave, unruffled visage seemed to slip, though he quickly pulled it back, "Not off the top of my head. As you can imagine, her diary is a complicated beast in itself. Indeed, I must be hurrying along now. I look forward to seeing you tomorrow, Mrs. Miller."

"Flora, please."

"My Flora!" Reggie, who had woken up when they stood, flapped his wings in agitation and then swooped across to Flora's shoulder.

"Such a charming pet," Martin said, though he had already put on his coat, hat and gloves, and was walking out of the door, his feet crunching on the frosted ground in leather-soled shoes that were clearly not suited to the wintery conditions.

"He has his moments," Flora replied as she stood in the doorway with Reggie, watching Martin get into a small car which looked like it was only one more trip away from the scrap heap. So at odds with his own pristine appearance, Flora thought, but then she couldn't imagine that Clarissa Cutter paid the man well. She didn't seem the sort to be generous of either mind or spirit. Flora squashed down the rising sense of alarm that the thought of meeting the woman in person evoked, and retreated to the safety of her little tearoom. With the radiators blasting out heat, it was a stark contrast to the freezing conditions outside.

"Amy, how are you?" Flora greeted her friend, who had arrived just before she was about to close up for the day, happy to see her looking fit and well after the worrying events of the other night.

"I'm feeling better, Flora, thank you so much for asking. I'm sorry I didn't make it up here yesterday, but Linda is back so we were giving the salon a clean and freshen up ready to re-open on Monday."

"Of course, I'm just glad to see the colour back in your cheeks. Take a seat, what can I get you?"

"Is the coffee machine still on? I'd love a cappuccino. Hello Reggie!" Amy turned her attention to the bird who had landed in the middle of her table and was now strutting towards her as if he owned the place.

"Welcome to the tearoom! She's a keeper!" Reggie was turning on all the charm and Amy giggled in return. Flora was glad to see the young woman come out of her shell a bit.

"Yes, I think I'll have a coffee with you," Flora said, smiling, "the monstrous machine and I have come to a truce, I think, as the last few I've made have been more than passable! Now, I have some scones that need eating, shall we have them with jam and cream and make an afternoon tea of it?"

"Oh, that sounds lovely, Flora, I've been looking after Lewis again today and I could do with some sugar to give me a boost of energy!"

"And how is the little chap? I hope his grandma is feeling better?"

"She is, thank you, and Lewis is looking forward to coming to the bookshop tomorrow. I may have promised to buy him a book."

"Oh, that's lovely. I do have some colouring sheets and crayons to keep the little ones occupied, and of course there's the cosy corner with beanbags and cuddly toys if they want to look at a book."

"It's so perfect, Flora, you've done a great job."

"We've done a great job, don't underestimate your own part in getting the place ready, Amy, I'm so grateful for your help."

Amy blushed as Flora prepared their drinks, and Reggie kept her entertained with his antics, spreading one wing and then the other, and pretending to hide his face behind the closed side.

"You're so funny, Reggie," Flora heard Amy whisper, as the bird hopped up onto the younger woman's hand and she brought him close to her face for a downy soft nuzzle.

"So cute!" Reggie chirped back, repeating one of the phrases he had heard many times from the Marshall girls.

Once the scones had been enjoyed and the two women had chatted about their latest reads, Flora remembered to ask Amy about meeting Clarissa at the coach house in the morning.

"You mean, just me? Oh, Flora, I'm not sure I can..."

"Well, of course, I'll understand if you don't want to," Flora could relate to Amy's anxiety, she certainly had more than a few butterflies herself.

"It's not that I don't want to, of course I'd like to do anything to help out, it's just I'm, I'm... not so good with people."

"Well, I think you're fine with people, just maybe lacking in a little confidence which I can certainly relate to. Why don't you have a think about it, chat to Gareth maybe, and then let me know this evening? Gareth could even be there with you if you like?" Flora didn't know why she hadn't thought of it before, of course Amy would feel better if Gareth was there with her, "You could leave Lewis at the bookshop with me, I'm sure the Marshall girls will keep him entertained!"

"Yes, that sounds like a plan, I'll speak to Gareth this evening and text you to confirm," Amy's face was clouded with sadness and Flora felt very guilty for having ruined her good mood.

"Is everything okay, Amy, I mean apart from demanding friends?" Flora tried to make light of it, but she couldn't deny she felt worried for her friend.

"I've just been feeling a bit out of sorts lately, and Gareth has been... well, a bit off."

"A bit off?" Flora asked gently.

"Yes, just distant, not his usual affectionate self. I tried to talk to him the other day, for example, about whether he knew of any artists, Nat's old friends who might have been able to help you out if the Cutter lady didn't come through, but he pretty much just blanked me. Said he was tired. I get the impression maybe he's going off me, and just doesn't know how to tell me," Amy's eyes filled with unshed tears and Flora reached out and took the younger woman's hand in hers.

Reggie, who had taken a perch on the back of one of the unused chairs at the table, cocked his head and looked intently from one to the other.

"Good bird," Amy whispered to reassure him, though her voice shook and her lip trembled.

Flora felt slightly out of her depth, and could only

speak from her own limited experience, "Well, I don't know how Gareth is feeling, perhaps he is simply tired from work, but I do know that I wish there had been more honesty in my marriage. Now, I make a point of speaking my truth and encouraging Adam to do the same. It saves any misunderstandings, I think. Perhaps you could just ask Gareth outright?"

Amy looked unsure, "I'm not very good with confrontation," she whispered.

"Well, maybe it needn't be a confrontation, just a chat?"

"Yes, I'll try to talk to him, maybe on Sunday, thank you," Amy whispered, giving Reggie's head one more stroke as she stood to leave.

"You're so welcome, and thank you so much for tomorrow, that's a weight off my mind! I'll leave the front door key for the coach house under the welcome mat outside. The ribbon cutting is scheduled for eleven o'clock, so I imagine if you're there by half past ten that should be fine."

"Will do," Amy said, and gave a weak smile which didn't reach the corners of her mouth let alone her eyes.

"She's a keeper!" Reggie squawked in Flora's ear as the two watched Amy walk away.

"She certainly is," Flora whispered back, though she had a sadness in the pit of her stomach which niggled her as she washed the dishes and closed the tearoom for the evening.

SEVEN

Flora grumbled as she searched for her mobile phone in the bottom of her handbag. The incessant ringing had disturbed a lovely conversation she was having with Adam about a possible holiday in Yorkshire in the spring time. Curled up on the sofa, with the tartan throw keeping them snug and the radio playing classic love songs in the background, Flora had finally been able to relax and forget about everything else but them, in their little cocoon.

"Shut yer mouth!" Reggie shrieked, woken suddenly by Flora's frantic searching just under his perch.

"Don't be rude!" Flora chided him, "You'd think you might have forgotten some of Harold's sayings by now!"

Reggie huffed with a flick of his head before shoving it back under his wing.

"Hello?" Flora finally found the cause of the noisy disturbance, though she couldn't imagine why anyone would be calling her at quarter to ten on a Friday night in winter.

"Hello, Mrs. Miller?" the clear-cut tones of Martin Loughbrough came through the other end, "I am so sorry to bother you."

He did indeed sound regretful, and Flora had a sinking feeling he may be calling to say that Clarissa was no longer coming the next day, though whether that would be such a bad thing, Flora was no longer sure, "Not at all, is everything okay?"

"Well, ah," the man cleared his throat, sounding thoroughly embarrassed as he tripped over his words uncharacteristically, "Well, Ms. Cutter has asked me to call, as she, ah, it is rather an indelicate matter I'm afraid."

Flora was losing patience and wished the man would just spit it out, "Please, Mr. Loughbrough…"

"Indeed, it is the, ah, the matter of payment, Mrs. Miller. It has not been made."

"Oh, I see," Flora let out the breath she had been holding.

"What is it?" Adam mouthed at her from the other side of the room.

Flora shrugged her shoulders and raised her free hand in a gesture of confusion in reply, before answering the man on the other end of the line, "When you didn't mention the money earlier, I assumed I would just be invoiced after the event," she said tersely.

"Ah, then it is indeed my error, Mrs. Miller, as I should have informed you that Ms. Cutter insists on, ah, requests payment before any engagement."

"I see, well, I'm not sure what she would like me to do about it now," Flora's feelings towards having this woman at her grand opening had now morphed from vague regret to abject remorse and discomfort.

Martin paused before replying, as if reining in his own temper, though Flora knew this was more likely to be aimed at his boss than her, "I can only apologise Flora, but Clarissa is insisting on an immediate bank transfer."

"Very well," Flora had little choice, she had invested too much time and headspace in this woman's visit to back out now. Even Adam had been roped in, buying the bottled spring water, tissues and hand cream from Morpeth and bringing them across with him, "two hundred pounds was it?"

"Quite so. Shall I email you the bank details?"

"Yes, otherwise she won't receive the money will she? Heaven forbid that she must wait till tomorrow!" Flora knew she was being churlish, but her temper was barely being kept in check now. Adam, having disappeared for a moment, came back into the room with a glass of red wine, and Flora was thankful that he could read her so well.

"Very well. I look forward to seeing you tomorrow morning," Martin ended the call with his usual formal tone, and Flora threw the offending phone back into her bag.

"Well, I really..!" Flora was about to explode, when Adam gave her a big hug and then handed her the wine, effectively diffusing the situation.

"By tomorrow lunchtime, this will be over and she'll be out of your life. You won't even have to think about her again," Adam said, following Flora into the kitchen where she opened her laptop to seek out Martin's email and make the payment.

"And that," Flora replied, "is the only thought keeping me going right now. That and you," she laid her head on his shoulder and felt thankful for Adam's solid reliability.

After very little sleep, Flora was dosed up on caffeine and had decided to take a walk up to Billy's bench before the day got started. It was not the first time she had visited since Christmas – far from it in fact. Whilst the big house felt foreboding and rather oppressive, so much so that she had halted all work on it, this little spot at the top of the rose garden always filled Flora with a sense of peace. She wondered if it had given the same sense of solitude and quiet to Billy and Mabel all the times they had shared this spot, and hoped that it had. Flora took in a deep breath of the clean air – so different from the London smog she had been used to – and then blew it out. It was so cold that she could see her breath as she exhaled, and the simple motion gave Flora a sense of pleasure. She would get through the coming day, as she had all others leading to this point, some a lot harder than this. After all, what did she need to do? Simply smile and welcome her guests, a small speech, that woman cutting the ribbon, tea and muffins with the reading of her first Reggie story and hopefully a few sales of other books in the shop and then all done and dusted.

The roses themselves were all dormant now, no buds showing in the wintery scene, but Flora recalled Billy's poem from the Christmas talent show, the seasons of life and how the roses would bloom again. The thought made Flora smile and brought further peace to her soul. Soon she would need to go back to the coach house to change into her outfit for the day and collect Reggie to take him to the tearoom with her, but for now Flora enjoyed the moment of quiet reflection.

She had laid her clothes on the bed ready, so a hot shower and get dressed, then she would be good to go. So, so tempted to wear blue, as it was her event after all, and Flora had never liked being told what to do – especially now she was free from her suffocating marriage – she decided instead on a beautiful two piece in emerald green. *Let the uppity Ms. Cutter keep her blues, she would never outshine this outfit*, Flora decided. Hand-made on Savile Row in London, the dress and matching bolero jacket had been made several years before, rather ironically for a court appearance in which Gregory had been pleading guilty to speeding. He had insisted Flora get dressed up to the nines for the occasion, and had taken her for a fancy lunch in The Savoy afterwards, claiming he cared little about the huge fine he had been landed with. Other than a quick trip to the dry cleaner's, it had hung in a wardrobe since then, and had survived the cull of Flora's clothes that she and Tanya had done a few months ago. It wasn't that the suit held particularly great memories, rather that it had been made to fit her, and Flora knew it looked as expensive as it had been. She had been unable to part with it.

Hot and sweaty, despite the shower she had just taken, Flora grappled with the side zip on her dress. Huffing and puffing, she was now lying diagonally across her bed, with Reggie watching her closely, from a safe distance. Even he knew not to disturb his companion when she was in this mood! Despite her efforts and contortions, the stupid zipper would only go halfway up, leaving Flora panting and furious.

"Damn hormones!" she said aloud, though in truth she knew her curvier figure was probably much more likely a result of being surrounded all day by cakes and baked goods, and by the sedentary life she led. This would not be remedied by Jazzercise alone! No, Flora knew a much stricter regime was called for. Starting tomorrow. For today, she reluctantly acknowledged with an angry growl, there was no way her emerald green beauty was going to fasten, let alone look passable.

"Clock's a ticking," Reggie said, in possibly his least helpful comment ever, Flora thought.

"I know!" she barked, looking at the alarm clock on her bedside table which showed half past eight. She should be at the tearoom by now. The muffins were being delivered from the patisserie in Whitley Bay, and there were a hundred and one other jobs to do.

Resignedly, Flora struggled out of the form-fitting dress and threw it over the small Victorian chair in the corner of the room.

"Grrr," she rushed through to the tiny box room, where she kept her second small wardrobe – the one with clothes that were not for everyday use. The pretty summer dresses were obviously a no-go, as were the black and grey business suits that Flora had kept for funerals and work meetings. The cocktail dresses and ballgowns, of which she had kept only three, were also discarded from consideration. The only option left was a floaty 1920s style number, in deep crimson, which had a dropped waist, light gauze which covered the shoulders in place of sleeves, and was adorned with sequins in the same deep red colour. It was more suited to acting a part at a murder mystery party than any form of sensible daytime attire, but Flora didn't care. She had to outshine Clarissa at all costs, and this would have to be the dress to do it!

Thankfully, given its boxier shape, this still fit well, and had the plus point of even skimming over Flora's new curves.

"My Flora! She's a corker!" Reggie exclaimed as Flora trudged back in to her bedroom to apply her make up and dry her hair.

"Thank you," Flora whispered, stroking his soft head, though in truth she felt more like crying than celebrating her small victory. She knew the outfit would garner some raised eyebrows, not least from the ladies of the W.I. in their tweed skirts and sensible brogues, but Flora no longer cared. If she was doing it, she was going to do it in style!

EIGHT

Calmed by a cup of Earl Grey and the rather blunt, but nonetheless complimentary words of Tanya, who simply asked where the red carpet was and made a whistling noise, Flora was feeling rather more positive when Adam arrived. Himself dressed smartly in beige chinos and a crisp white shirt, the man clearly knew better than to comment much on Flora's appearance. Instead, the raised eyebrow which conveyed his initial shock was quickly replaced by a peck on her cheek and a whispered, "You look lovely!"

"Thank you, this was a rather… last minute choice."

"I think you're beautiful whatever you wear," Adam said into her ear, causing Flora to blush.

"Aw you lovebirds, so sweet," Tanya said, setting the

muffins out on cake stands.

"You sexy beast!" Reggie added from his perch, which had been moved to sit beside his portrait for the duration of the morning's events.

It was Adam's turn to blush now, just as the door opened and Martin walked in. With Tanya back in the tearoom side, and only Flora to see in Adam's arms, Martin looked uncomfortable, "Do excuse me, I was just instructed by Clarissa to come and see if everything is… oh, I am so sorry," the man blushed and began to back out.

"Don't be silly!" Flora quickly left Adam's embrace and hurried across to stop her visitor from leaving, "Was there something else we forgot yesterday?"

"Well, the thing is, ah, Clarissa was worrying that the scissors for cutting the ribbon might be rather heavy and interfere with her manicure." Martin raised an eyebrow as if he himself thought the notion ridiculous.

Flora thought it strange that an artist would have manicured fingernails, but then the whole outfit colour thing was evidence that the woman put great store in her appearance. That was the least of Flora's worries, however, when she suddenly realised that in focusing on all the minutiae of the event, she had indeed forgotten the one thing that mattered – something to cut the ribbon.

"Oh my goodness!" Flora put her hand to her throat, causing Adam to rush over in immediate concern.

"What is it, love?"

"I forgot to order the ceremonial scissors. You know, the big ones that are only sharp enough to do the job but look the part."

"Well, don't fret," Adam said, as Martin stood wringing his hands together uncomfortably, "let's think about this logically. What scissors do we have?"

"Just the ones I use in the kitchen for cutting wrappings and such like, and in my purse just nail scissors, nothing grand enough."

"What about the butcher in the village?"

"Eugh, no," Flora tapped her hand on the nearest bookshelf as she thought.

"Is there a local tailor? Those shears are normally bigger," Martin asked.

"No, sadly not," Flora replied, "oh, however, Jean who owns the local shop does quilting and crafts. Maybe she would have some tailoring shears for cutting cloth!" Flora rushed through to the tearoom to grab her phone from her bag.

"Crisis averted," Flora said, smiling widely, and swishing through to the bookshop, the beads on her dress jangling as she walked. The high red sandals over slippery black tights had probably not been the best choice, given that she was going to be on her feet all day, but Flora had not had time to give them much thought before rushing out the door earlier.

"You found some?" Martin asked

"I did indeed, Jean to the rescue. We must just make a point to know where they are at all times and keep them behind the counter out of reach of the little ones, as Jean says they are very sharp."

"Perfect," Martin smiled, as his pocket began to vibrate and the commanding tones of the national anthem filled the room, "Ah, that'll be Clarissa, I'd better take it."

Flora and Adam exchanged a look, but said nothing as a shrill voice on the other end of the call seemed to be chewing Martin's ear off. The poor man barely got a word in before a shrieked "Not acceptable" was heard and the line suddenly went silent.

"Well?" Flora asked, her hands on her hips.

"Ah, Ms. Cutter says she is at your tiny, ah, compact house and there is no-one there to meet her."

"Well, it is only quarter past ten, Amy should be there shortly," Flora replied, her exasperation beginning to show in both her tone and the way she began to brush invisible pieces of lint from her dress. Adam put his arm around her shoulders and hugged her close to his side.

"Worry not, love, she'll be fine waiting in her car until Amy arrives," he kissed the top of Flora's head gently.

Apparently uncomfortable with the small display of affection, Martin placed his hat back on his head and headed out the door, "I'll just walk along and pacify her. This way is it?"

When Flora had confirmed the path, she took a deep breath in, "This doesn't bode well. She's angry before she even gets here!" she whispered.

Adam had no words of comfort this time, which gave Flora the distinct impression that he agreed.

Early as always, Betty and Harry arrived with Jean and

the tailors' shears which were stored safely behind the counter in the tearoom. Happy to wait for the main event with a hot drink and a muffin, the trio were soon joined by Shona and Aaron, and then the vicar and his family. Lastly, little Lewis was dropped off by a very harassed looking Gareth, who said he was running late to meet Amy at the coach house. This news added to Flora's sinking feeling, as surely Amy must have had to deal with the woman by herself for at least twenty minutes already.

Just as Flora had greeted Lizzie, and introduced her to everyone as the lady who had painted the magnificent portrait of Reggie, the door flew open and a tall, angular woman appeared, her face the picture of misery.

"What do you mean by sending this snivelling girl to meet me?" she asked of no one in particular, until her eyes settled on Flora, "You, you in the ridiculous fancy dress, I assume you are the owner of this charade?"

Flora stepped forward, holding her hand up to silence Adam, who looked like he was about to give the woman a piece of his mind.

"Clarissa Cutter, I presume," Flora said, as a sobbing Amy arrived, with Gareth and Martin hot on the women's heels.

"I'm so sorry," Amy sobbed, "She was spraying this perfume all around, you see, and the smell of it was so overpowering, I had to run off to be sick. Then she started shrieking at me, and my head was spinning."

"You poor thing," Tanya said, putting an arm around Amy's trembling shoulders.

"Indeed," Flora hid the quiver in her voice very well, as she looked Clarissa straight in the eyes, "I asked Amy to meet you, which she was kind enough to do, not to be subject to your harsh criticism. How dare you upset my friend!"

"Well, the scent she is referring to is Chanel, the stupid girl clearly has no taste! And I have never been spoken to like…"

"Oh, I'm sure you have," Gareth cut in, his face a perfect picture of fury. His cheeks were red and his eyes bulged, whilst Flora worried at the sight of his hands balled into fists at his sides.

Adam must've taken in the man's appearance too, for he suggested he take him into the tearoom for a cuppa. Gareth declined with a curt shake of the head, and kept his gaze focused on Clarissa.

"I recognise you!" he shouted, "You're the woman

who was one of my Natalie's tutors in art college. You never did stop criticising her, even when she graduated and was working freelance. Whenever she had a picture in the gallery in Alnwick you would write a piece about it, pulling her down. Whenever she got her confidence up, there you were to put her back in her place, as you saw it!" Gareth made what could only be described as a growl and Martin stepped between he and Clarissa.

"Well, this is quite the scene!" Edwina Edwards scoffed as she and the good doctor arrived, with perfect timing as always, to see Flora's hopes of a smooth, first class event blown into smithereens.

"Oh, put a sock in it, Edwina!" Betty said, from the crowd that had formed around the doorway to the bookshop.

"What have I missed?" Lily could be heard whispering from the back, late as always as the farm kept her busy from dawn till dusk.

"Just a strange, wiry looking woman who has upset our Amy and needs to be put out on her backside," Tanya answered, loud enough for all to hear.

"Well, I, I don't think that's necessary," Martin interjected, only to hold his silence again as Gareth glared at him.

There was nothing for it, but for Flora to take charge and diffuse the situation, "I think it's been made quite clear that you're not welcome here, as you can see, there are children who don't need to witness this," she stood face to face with Clarissa now, though a good few inches shorter. The woman looked down her pointed nose at Flora with pure disdain, flicked her perfectly-coiffed hair off her shoulders, and stood her ground.

"Children? Martin, why was I not told there would be children in attendance?" she snarled, as if Flora had mentioned vermin and not little people, "Where are the press? The Gazette and the Chronicle," she asked, clearly not fazed by the sheer amount of animosity that was being levelled at her, "I'll give my interview before I leave."

A small, rotund man, with a balding pate and greasy combover pushed his way through the small group, "Donald Percy, Madam, from 'What's on the Rise in Baker's Rise.'"

"From where? What is this sweaty, fat little man talking about? I only deal with the big players. Now, where is the representative from the Courier?"

A whisper went around the room and for a moment all fell silent, until the flutter of green feathers swooped over them and hovered directly over Clarissa's head, "You old trout!" Reggie screeched, and Flora secretly hoped he would drop one of his stinky parcels on the woman's head. No such luck, however, as she spun on her heel and made to leave.

"Agh! What is that rude green bird doing here? I don't work with animals!" Clarissa was shrieking now, in a grand repetition of Reggie's own tone, "You'll be hearing from my solicitor! Martin, with me!"

"Well, I don't know what to say, I'm just…" Martin shook his head sadly in Flora's direction, the poor man looked mortified, though he made no move to follow his employer.

"Betty, can you look after Amy, please? I need to calm down," Gareth said, heading out through the door that Clarissa had just exited.

"Ah, Miss Cutter, I was hoping to have a word!"

"What on earth is Phil doing?" Flora asked, as the schoolteacher could be seen chasing after the woman, who was stomping across the gravel driveway.

"He said something about getting her to put in a good

word for him in literary circles," Harry said, shaking his head as if the other man had really lost the plot this time.

"Well good luck to him with that one," Flora muttered, as she turned to face everyone assembled, "Thank you for coming, I think we can dispense with the formalities, let's just say the bookshop is open!"

NINE

"Well, I guess that's that, then, no hope of having her illustrate my books now," Flora lamented to Adam as the Marshall girls ran around the bookshop pretending to be spaceships, encouraging Aaron and Lewis to do the same. Soon the other schoolchildren who were there joined in, and Reggie himself, until Tanya put a stop to it.

"Cease, little ones, Flora I think it is time for the story, no?"

"It certainly is," Flora replied, trying to put a brave face on it. The show must go on, after all.

As Flora sat on a beanbag, and the children huddled around her in hushed anticipation, Lizzie walked over to Martin, who still hovered in the doorway, apparently unsure as to whether he should stay or go.

"Martin, Martin Loughbrough isn't it? We were at art college together. I don't know if you remember me, it's Lizzie," a faint blush spread up from the woman's neck, almost matching the colour of the scarf she had tied as a headband around her curls.

"Lizzie, yes, yes of course, I remember you were in some classes with Clarissa and I. We came to your twenty-first birthday party. You and she weren't quite friends though, if I recall."

"No, you could say that, and haven't been since either! She has a distinctly negative view of my work, in fact, one which she's more than willing to share at every possible opportunity, both locally and nationally," Lizzie paused and took a deep breath, as if trying to calm herself, "But I remember what a talented artist you were. Did I hear Flora correctly, that you're now working as Clarissa's personal assistant?"

"Well, yes, we had always kept in touch, then we met up again at a gallery about a decade ago and she invited me on board so to speak," Martin flushed and tugged at his cravat as if the air in the room was suddenly too hot, "anyway, I'd better be finding the woman in question, need to pour oil on troubled waters, you know how it is."

Lizzie could just imagine, and raised an eyebrow as

she watched him hurry out. How strange, she thought, that such a talented artist should end up doing another creator's admin for a living. But then, he had always trailed around after Clarissa with puppy dog eyes, even at college – much to Lizzie's own chagrin – she recalled.

"And that is how Reggie met an alien," Flora finished her story with a flourish and the children all cheered.

"Another one, Miss Flora," Evie asked, and soon the chant was taken up by them all.

"Let me get a cup of tea and then we'll see," Flora said, finding it rather more difficult than she'd like to admit extricating herself from the beanbag. In the end, Adam grabbed her hand and literally hauled her out. Not her finest moment, Flora thought, but then that could be said for the whole morning, to be honest.

"And then she went on a rant about amateur authors," Phil was in the middle of a long moan when Flora re-entered the tearoom, and she didn't need two guesses to know who he was referring to. Sidestepping the table which he shared with Dr. and Mrs. Edwards, Flora instead took a seat with Tanya, Lily, Amy, Shona, Jean and Betty. Harry was having a browse in the bookshop, Pat Hughes was on duty, Stan had been held up at the farm, and Will was full of cold, so it was only the women who gathered.

Looking at the all-female group rather apprehensively, Adam muttered something about helping Harry look for books and then disappeared back the way they had come. Flora smiled, for what felt like the first time since she had been sat on Billy's bench that morning.

"Aye, get yerself sat down lass," Betty pulled a chair from a nearby table for Flora to join them, "what a morning, eh!"

"Yes, it was bordering on farcical wasn't it," Flora accepted the cup of tea Tanya offered her gratefully, "and I'm so sorry, Amy, how are you feeling now?"

"Just a little queasy," Amy replied, "but better than earlier, please don't worry Flora, you weren't to know I'd feel sick like that. Smells never normally set me off."

Flora caught Tanya and Betty sharing a knowing look, but wasn't party to their meaning. She made a mental note to ask Tanya about it later, "Well, I never should have left you to deal with that witch in the first place," Flora said solemnly.

"She was awful," Jean agreed, quietly crocheting whilst the rest of them spoke.

"That's an understatement," Shona said, as the vicar and Sally emerged from the bookshop, three squirming girls held between them.

"We'd better be getting back," Sally said, "Megan is overtired and they're all overexcited, thank you so much for the invitation, Flora."

"Oh, I hope you had some tea and muffins?" Flora knew that was probably irrelevant given everything else that had gone on, but politeness prevailed.

"Yes, yes, thank you. I'll be back in on Monday afternoon with the girls after school and we can catch up then."

"Of course," Flora replied, though she was distracted by Gareth emerging behind them from the bookshop. Though somewhat more relaxed in body, his face still bore the black look from earlier. He sidestepped the church family and went straight to Amy, who welcomed him with a smile that looked half relief and half worry.

Distracted by seeing the Marshall family out, Flora didn't catch the conversation which followed, only that

Amy and Gareth were leaving.

"I think Amy needs a rest," Gareth said tersely.

"Of course, and I am so sorry, Amy," Flora was compelled to keep reiterating it, she felt so awful.

"Please don't worry, Flora," Amy whispered, as she put on her coat and Gareth took her hand, "Oh, Gareth, my car is still at the coach house!"

"Is it okay if I walk Amy up to get her car and then come back for Lewis?" Gareth asked.

"By all means, he was playing with Reggie last time I saw him," Flora said, happy she could help in some small way, "we'll keep a close eye on him."

"Thank you," and with that the couple left, closely followed by Shona who had to get back to the pub with Aaron, and Jean who was expecting a delivery of yarns.

"I'll give you a lift into the village," Lily kindly offered Shona and Jean, "I'm passing through on the way to the farm anyway."

And suddenly the place seemed a lot quieter, and Flora didn't feel the euphoria she had hoped to experience once the event was over. Sure, she had sold a few books, and everyone who had promised to come had shown up, but it could hardly be called a resounding success – not a success on any scale, really – and Flora felt like having a good mope about it.

"Chin up, love," Adam said, coming to wave the others off with her, "it could've been worse."

"I'd like to know how," Flora replied, though in truth she didn't wish to know how at all.

"My book!" Reggie chirped, as Lewis showed him the pictures in a farmyard board book. It wasn't one of Flora's stories about him, of course, but the parrot couldn't tell and Flora had been working on teaching him how to say 'book' for weeks now in the hope he would say it at this opening event and wow everyone.

"Oh well," Flora said to Adam as they stood watching the pair in the bookshop, "I guess I should be happy he was listening to me all those times after all. He still uses far too many of Harold's phrases for my liking!"

Just as Adam was about to reply, the door burst open and Gareth rushed in, Amy's limp form in his arms. It must have started raining, as he was soaked in the heavy drizzle, but it was his eyes which struck Flora first. They were as wild as any she had ever seen.

"Quick, detective," was all the man could say as he struggled to catch his breath.

"Amy!" Flora shrieked, wondering only for a second why he would ask for a detective when they clearly needed a doctor. Sadly, the Edwards couple had already left, as had everyone apart from Betty, Harry and Tanya.

"She's okay, I think. Fainted. Blood, everywhere," Gareth spoke in a staccato manner which was barely comprehensible to Flora's ears. Adam, however, seemed to understand the man.

"Flora, see to Amy. Gareth come with me," he said, as Gareth laid Amy on the nest of beanbags and both men rushed out the door.

"Blood!" Betty said coming through from the tearoom, her hearing lightning-quick when she wanted it to be. Amy, on closer inspection however, seemed to have not a drop of blood on her.

The young woman was already coming round as Flora, Betty and Tanya leaned over her. Harry had quickly taken little Lewis into the tearoom for some cake and juice, so there were no little eyes watching them other than Reggie's.

"Flora?" Amy's voice sounded hoarse and dry, as she struggled to work out her surroundings.

"You take a rest there for a minute," Betty said, "then you can tell us all about it."

Betty was never one to be patient when it came to getting information, but Flora was more concerned with making sure Amy was okay, "Does anywhere hurt, Amy?"

Tanya and Betty shared another of their secret looks from earlier, but Flora was still in the dark as to what they meant.

"No, no, I think I'm fine," Amy said, then as if something had just jumped into her mind, she burst into tears.

"What is it? A pain?" Flora asked, worried.

"A memory. It was that scent, the perfume from earlier, I could smell it all of a sudden when we were walking back and it made me wretch on the path up to your house. But when I leant into the bushes to be sick, there she was!"

"There who was?" all three women asked in unison.

"The artist, Ms. Cutter, covered in blood!"

A collective inhalation of breath was broken only by Reggie, worried by the atmosphere in the room, and shrieking "Secrets and Lies!" three times on shrill repeat.

"Desist silly bird!" Tanya chided him, whilst Betty pressed for more details.

"In the bush, you say? And was she dead?"

"Betty!" Flora whispered, "I'm sure Amy doesn't want to relive the moment!"

"I couldn't if I tried," Amy said, "I think I must've passed out then and the next I know I'm here with you."

Flora lay Adam's wool winter coat over the young woman who was shivering even in her own outdoor coat and cast a worried look to the other two, who clearly shared her concern. Whatever had happened, it couldn't be good. No, not good at all.

TEN

It was some twenty minutes later, when neither of the two men had returned, that Flora heard the first sirens rushing through the village and up the hill. The emergency vehicles must've taken the side route straight to the coach house, as they didn't arrive at the bookshop, and the noise simply stopped after a short while. The silence stretched out between the small group, uncomfortably so, with only the hum of Harry's voice reading to Lewis in the tearoom next door providing any relief.

"Gareth!" Amy croaked.

"Shh, I'm sure he's fine," Betty said quickly, too quickly to calm anyone's nerves.

"I will make us more tea," Tanya said reverently, as if the drink was an elixir which could restore calm in any situation.

Flora gently helped Amy to a sitting position, and they all made their way slowly into the tearoom, with Reggie following close behind. Flora noticed that he hadn't let her out of his sight since the commotion began, and grateful she was for it. After the stress and heartache of having him taken away from her before Christmas, albeit for a few days, she had kept him especially close by ever since.

"There we go," Tanya said with false cheeriness, as she served them all cups of hot, sweet tea from a huge vintage teapot.

"Perfect, let's have those leftover muffins, shall we? Keep our spirits up," Betty said, resorting to comfort food which had admittedly been Flora's own thoughts exactly. Any notions of a health and fitness regime were totally forgotten now as she savoured the flavour of the treat, realising she hadn't even managed to taste one of the delicious muffins until now. The day had turned into a wet, dark afternoon, and Flora shivered at the sight of the rain hammering against the window. She really wished she had worn trousers and a smart jumper instead of this ridiculous dress. Never mind, she would soon be at home, showered, changed and warm beside the fire. Or so Flora kept telling herself. In reality, she had a sinking feeling the path to her little cottage may be impassable for quite some time.

Amy was still as white as a sheet, though was thankfully no longer shivering. It was then that Flora realised the young woman still had Adam's coat draped around her shoulders – which meant that he himself was outside in the rain with no covering. She fervently hoped that he'd managed to pop into the coach house with the spare key she'd given him a few weeks ago, and borrowed one of her waterproofs. If not, he was going to be freezing and drenched by the time she saw him next.

It was after another round of hot tea, and some carrot cake to keep their spirits up, that the door finally opened and Adam appeared. His wet hair was plastered against his forehead but he was at least wearing a thick hi-vis police jacket as protection from the weather.

"Adam!" Flora exclaimed, jumping up to greet him. Even Reggie seemed relieved to have someone to break the thick atmosphere in the little tearoom, as he rose from his perch in a maelstrom of green feathers, rushing straight at Adam and shrieking "At last!" which echoed Flora's own sentiments perfectly.

"What's the news?" Betty asked, getting straight to the

heart of the matter. No doubt she wanted the warmth of her own hearth too, but Flora knew she wouldn't leave until she had all the details. Gossip wasn't a fair word, though it was probably accurate! Betty loved nothing better than having the inside scoop to share with her friends in the W.I. over lunch. Harry tiptoed out of the bookshop, indicating with a whisper that Lewis had finally fallen asleep on one of the beanbags. The older man looked tired and had worry lines even over and above his usual wrinkles. Flora imagined they must all look wrung out with the stress and uncertainty of it all.

"Well," Adam said, once he had divested himself of his dripping coat and gratefully accepted a cup of coffee from Tanya, who knew he preferred that over tea any day, "well, it's not good news, I'm afraid. To put it bluntly, there's been another murder."

"Clarissa," even saying the word gave Flora an awful sense of dread and foreboding.

"What happened to her?" Harry asked the question on everyone's lips.

"Stabbed, I'm afraid," Adam didn't elaborate further.

Suddenly a low keening sound began and everyone turned to Amy, who thus far had been sitting so quietly at the table that Flora had almost forgotten she was there.

"Amy!" Tanya jumped up and put her arm around their friend's shaking shoulders.

"Wh- where- where is Gareth?" she managed to say between trembling lips.

"Ah, well…" Flora could tell that Adam would rather be anywhere right now than having to impart more bad news, especially to the fragile young woman before them, but he pressed on in a very professional manner, "Gareth has been taken by my colleagues, detectives Blackett and McArthur, to the station in Morpeth. Just to help with enquiries, you understand, as it was the two of you who found the body. He hasn't been arrested or anything like that."

"Nooo!" Amy was shrieking now, and Reggie came to hide on Flora's lap, though she was without her usual cardigan or jumper for him to snuggle underneath.

"It's okay," Adam came to crouch in front of Amy so that he was on eye level with her, and spoke softly, "really, it is normal procedure as he found the body, they need to take a formal statement that's all. No doubt they'll want a chat with you too, when you're feeling up to it."

"But what about his outburst earlier, surely that will go against him?" Tanya voiced what the others were thinking but had the tact and sensitivity not to say.

"I'm not officially on the case, too close to the situation yet again," Adam forestalled any further questions expertly.

"Well, at least that awful woman won't be making any more cutting remarks – she certainly got the point!" Tanya obviously couldn't help herself, but her words caused poor Amy's sobbing to increase dramatically, earning the policeman's wife a glare from Flora.

"Anyway, on to practicalities," Adam said, standing up and ignoring Tanya's comments, "Tanya, if you could see Amy and Lewis home to her parents' house, I would be very grateful. Betty and Harry, would it be okay for Flora and Reggie to stay with you overnight? I'm on duty over in Morpeth this evening. The forensics team have erected a tent over the area encompassing that part of the footpath to the coach house and are also using the driveway and combing the whole area, so the cottage itself won't be accessible until tomorrow afternoon at the earliest. Hopefully, we can find a way that bypasses that part of the path."

With this all agreed, Flora told Betty she would be along later, citing the need to clear up, though in fact she just wanted to speak to Adam alone.

"I can help you tidy, it is my job now after all," Tanya offered.

"No, no, I think it's best if Amy gets home as quickly as possible," Adam interjected, "I think a nice lie down is in order. Then she'll have her parents to help with Lewis until Gareth gets back."

"Good plan," Flora agreed, and busied herself helping little Lewis get his coat and hat on.

When she had waved them all off, and Reggie had retreated back to his perch, happy that whatever had caused the strangeness seemed to have passed, Flora found Adam behind the counter in the tearoom. Not a normal occurrence, she questioned it immediately.

"Well, this is just between you and me love, really I would be compromising the case if the information went any further, but we think the murder weapon may be scissors or something similarly pointed and sharp. We couldn't find anything fitting that description on an initial scan of the site, though."

"No!" Flora instantly made the mental connection between what he was saying and where Adam was looking, "Please tell me Jean's tailoring shears are still there, unused and where we put them."

"Well, you can come and have a look, see if I've missed them, but as far as I can see – no."

"Oh my goodness," Flora said, rushing behind the counter and searching the shelves below for any sign of the large scissors. Of course, she found nothing. They were too big an item to miss easily, so they had to acknowledge that the shears were missing.

"Well, that puts a worse slant on things," Adam said.

"For Gareth, you mean?"

"Mhm, and for everyone who was here, really. All will need to be questioned," Adam's countenance was grave, and Flora leaned into him for reassurance.

Accepting the warmth of Adam's embrace gratefully, Flora whispered, "When we were all transfixed by Clarissa's rude entrance, anyone could have snook back here."

"Quite right," Adam agreed, "but only a few would have had a motive to do so."

"That's true," Gareth wasn't the only one who came to Flora's mind then, with Lizzie and even Phil and that little man from the local newsletter having reasons to dislike the now-deceased woman, "though given her temperament, realistically she could have made many enemies along the way!"

"Absolutely," Adam nodded against the top of Flora's head, "Blackett and McArthur will have their work cut out for them. I'll of course have to keep working the case in Alnwick of the other artist."

"Do you think the deaths could be connected?" Flora looked up at him.

"Possibly, we'll see. Now, about this dress..."

"Oh, I had forgotten about this stupid thing!" Flora looked down at herself, feeling ridiculous, "How can I spend the next twenty-four hours in this?"

"Well, hopefully Betty will have something you can borrow, or Jean maybe?" Flora thought she saw the hint of a smirk pass over Adam's lips, but it was gone before she could be sure.

"I guess that's the least of my worries," Flora whispered, resting her head on Adam's shoulder once again and thankful for the comfort of his arms around her, "I can't believe it. Another murder in Baker's Rise!"

ELEVEN

Flora woke with a start, unsure of where she was. Then she opened her eyes and saw the small bird staring at her from her pillow, the chintzy curtains behind him framing a window sill full of dainty ornaments, and it all came flooding back.

"My Flora," Reggie chirped and nuzzled his head into Flora's cheek. She drew her hand out from under the warm blanket and into the cold morning air, and returned the gesture with a small chest rub. Reggie puffed out his feathers under her fingers and cocked his head to one side, giving Flora the distinct impression that he was gauging her current state. His perceptive little eyes focused on hers, and Flora spoke gently to reassure him.

"Good bird, Reggie, good bird, all fine, all fine."

"Fine, fine," Reggie sang back and hopped from one foot to the other.

Seeing him this perky gave Flora a feeling of relief. Whilst her hosts had been very kind, offering her the fold-out bed in Harry's study and even a cotton nightdress of Betty's, Reggie had been very unsettled without any of his normal home comforts like his perch, cage or seed tray. Flora had made him a fruit salad, and Jean had provided some wild bird seed from the shop, but Reggie had simply picked at it all morosely, adding to Flora's worries of the previous evening. Since she herself had barely eaten more than a few mouthfuls of Betty's homemade shepherd's pie herself, however, Flora figured she could understand how the little guy felt.

As Betty was much shorter and rounder than Flora, it had quickly been established that any daywear of hers would not be suitable, so Jean had come to the rescue again. A similar height to Flora, though slightly smaller in frame, and not knowing how long Flora would be without her own things, Jean had been able to provide a couple of pairs of trousers and some warm, knitted jumpers. Anything would be an improvement on the dress, Flora had decided, though she had to admit she didn't relish the thought of attending church in the borrowed ensemble.

Nevertheless, to church they did go, leaving Reggie shut in the study and Tina in the sitting room, lest the two animals should have a disagreement whilst they were out. Thankfully, the rain had stopped and they walked the short distance around the duck pond quickly, with Harry taking the opportunity to talk about some of the estate's accounts. Flora's mind, however, was on other things, and she couldn't follow his detailing of rents and interest earned.

"Harry, thank you so much, but I hope you don't mind if we leave this till a weekday? Perhaps you could come by the tearoom? My brain is a bit foggy today."

"Of course, my dear, I should have thought. I doubt that sofa-bed was very comfortable, was it? You'll be glad to get back to the coach house."

"I will indeed! Thank you."

"Has there been any news from Adam?" Betty asked.

"No, other than a goodnight text, though he's not working on the case so he won't be privy to any information."

"Shame," Betty said, clearly disappointed that her

information well had dried up for now.

The church was fuller than normal, which would no doubt make the vicar happy, Flora thought, but she herself had the sneaking suspicion that it was more likely that people had come to gossip. The news of the murder would have spread like wildfire through the village, as things do in small, rural communities, and Flora kept her head low to avoid any uncomfortable questions. Betty did the rounds before the service, though, and Flora could hear her moving from pew to pew and speaking in a stage whisper which would have been comical at any other time.

Just before the service was due to start, Amy came in quietly through the side door with her parents, and Flora jumped up to greet her friend.

"Amy! I didn't think to see you here! How are you faring?"

"A little better, thank you Flora," Amy said, coming to sit next to Flora whilst her parents went to find friends nearer the back, "especially since Gareth is back at his home now."

"Really? That is good news!"

"Yes, he came for Lewis late last night and we didn't

have a chance to talk, but at least he's been released."

"Indeed!" Flora breathed a sigh of relief as the organ began the first hymn and Betty rushed to take her seat beside them.

It was somewhere between the sermon and the prayers – Flora may have had a little doze while the vicar was speaking, though she would never admit as much – that there was a commotion from the back of the building. Reverend Marshall stopped speaking and everyone turned around to see detectives Blackett and McArthur walking down the aisle, bold as brass, and stopping beside Phil Drayford's pew.

"He must be next!" Betty said, with rather more glee than the situation warranted. To be fair, the rest of the congregation buzzed with a similar excitement at having the monotony of the day broken by an unusual, noteworthy event, and it took the good vicar several attempts, and a lot of patience, to get everyone focused back on him once the trio had left. He himself seemed to realise that he had lost his audience's attention for that day, and rushed through the final parts of the service, much to the delight of his little daughters, who had their coats on ready to leave before the final 'Amen' was even spoken.

Flora had hoped to have a chance to talk some more

with Amy after the service, but her parents sensibly whisked her away to avoid the curious glances and whispers of some of their neighbours. Instead she walked back to Betty's for Sunday lunch with Betty, Harry, Jean and Shona, with Aaron running ahead of them. To be honest, the last thing Flora wanted was to keep being sociable, but as she had no choice she plastered a smile on her face and made the best of it.

With Adam's help early that evening, Flora forged a new path around the back of the coach house, and down the side of the little building to reach the front door. Thankfully Reggie travelled on her shoulder, or flew above them, so she didn't have to worry about him.

"Home! Cosy!" he squawked as Flora unlocked the front door. She had deliberately kept her eyes averted from the white tent and vans parked behind her, as this whole situation was anxiety-inducing enough without seeing the reality of it up close. Thankfully, the heating had come on automatically from the thermostat the previous evening and early that morning, so her home was still quite warm. Adam went in ahead to check the place over, just in case, and then lit the fire while Flora made them both a cup of coffee.

"I'm sorry I'll have to drink this and run," Adam said, "I've left my car at Betty's and I've got to work tonight."

"I understand. Any news on… anything?" Flora asked, trying but failing to be subtle.

"Only that they've interviewed Phil Drayford, which you knew already. I would expect a visit yourself very shortly," Adam said, then tried to soften the information with a quick kiss. It wasn't a shock to Flora anyway, she was beginning to learn how these things worked now.

"Well, as long as they don't turn up while I'm in the bath, that's fine," Flora replied, "I'm desperate to get out of these clothes and into my own. It was very kind of Jean, but I have to admit this wool is a bit itchy! And I feel like I've earned a good, long soak."

Flora gave a rueful smile and Adam smiled back, it was a shared moment of unspoken promises. Of things they wished they could say, if time allowed and circumstances were different. But they weren't and time together was fleeting at the moment, so before Flora even had time to feel sad or dwell too deeply, Adam was gone and it was just her and her little green friend again.

TWELVE

When the doorbell rang just as she was putting on her cosiest, fluffiest pyjamas, despite it being only quarter past seven, Flora was sorely tempted to just ignore it. She had a sinking feeling it would be Phil Drayford – not because she could imagine him having anything he needed to say to her in particular, but rather because every time in recent months that she had opened the door to a surprise visitor, it had always been Phil. At the incessant ringing, Flora quickly pulled on a fleecy robe and some rather fetching bed socks and reluctantly stomped down her little hallway.

"The fool has arrived!" Reggie shrieked as he followed Flora's path, as if even he assumed it would be Phil come to disturb their peace.

Imagine Flora's shock, then, when it turned out not to be Phil after all, but rather Martin Loughbrough who stood on the doorstep, looking gaunt and woebegone. His usually dapper appearance had gone decidedly awry, and now he stood in a crumpled suit which was missing his signature cravat. Martin's hat, too, seemed to have disappeared since the previous day and his hair stood up as if he had run his fingers through it one too many times. His winter gloves were wet and muddy, matching his shoes which had also lost their usual sheen.

Despite his unkempt appearance, it was the fact that he was there at all that shocked Flora the most, "How did you even get here, Martin?" she asked.

"Oh, er, I left my car on the lane and walked up the driveway here, it seems to be clear," and so it did. As Flora peered cautiously past him, even despite the darkness of the coming night she could make out that the vans had disappeared. Even Clarissa's car seemed to have been towed away.

"And why did you come?" Flora's politeness filter seemed to be on the blink, as she was being as blunt as Tanya right now and couldn't seem to either help it or to care.

"Sorry, Flora, sorry, I wanted to see where it… where

she… the police came to visit me earlier today, you see, with all their questions, and they said it happened here. I only knew that she was ignoring me yesterday evening… or so I thought… do you know anything more about the investigation?"

Flora noticed that the man's eyes were glassy and his hands trembling where he clasped them fiercely together in front of him. A strong odour of whisky fumes wafted towards her when he spoke, and she wondered whether Martin should have driven at all, "Ah, I'm so sorry, Martin, I didn't think to call you, in all the confusion and changes of plans, it didn't even cross my mind that you might not know. Right now, I probably know less than you do."

They stood there awkwardly then, with neither speaking and just the persistent sniffing from Martin's nose to distract them. Eventually, Flora felt she had no choice but to ask, "Would you like to come in?"

"Yes, yes, thank you, if you don't mind, I don't want to be a bother, it was just such a shock. I thought maybe she was giving me the silent treatment you see and then…" Martin's voice cracked and he paused to take a shaky breath. Flora directed him into the sitting room where the log burner was doing a grand job of keeping the place toasty. Reggie didn't seem to know what to make of the new visitor, and was sizing him up from the safety of Flora's shoulder. Keen to forestall any potential outbursts from the bird, Flora took him into the kitchen with her while she made them both some sweet tea, and gave him a couple of juicy green grapes to keep him quiet. His appetite apparently fully restored from the previous evening, Reggie accepted these gratefully, and sat with them happily on the kitchen table.

"So," Flora began, when she and Martin was sitting with their drinks, and the man seemed to be more in control of his emotions, "I had assumed that you had gone after Clarissa yesterday when you left the bookshop?"

"I planned to, I meant to, but… well in truth I was angry with her for the way she embarrassed me, and herself, and for the way she spoke to everyone. I couldn't honestly face her, and I assumed she would be in touch with me very quickly to vent anyway. I'm normally the one who's subject to her rages…" Martin paused and took a sip of his tea, and Flora got the distinct impression he had stopped himself deliberately before he said too much, "anyway, I would never speak ill of the dead. Suffice to say, I thought to put off the inevitable for as long as possible. We had come in separate cars, if you recall, as I was coming to see you in the tearoom first, so I simply drove away home. I figured I would face her when we were both in a better frame of mind."

"I see, and then she simply didn't call?"

"Exactly, radio silence which for Clarissa was… well, unheard of. She was nothing if not vocal about her grievances, as you yourself are all too aware, Flora. I thought she was maybe blaming me in some way for the manner in which things had panned out and gone downhill, or wanted to punish me for something, which wouldn't have been unusu… anyway, I thought to simply play her at her own game and see who could hold out the longest. The next I know, the detectives were on my doorstep this morning!"

Though Flora thought the relationship between Clarissa and Martin sounded unusual at best, and extremely unhealthy at worst, she gave no indication of this, simply taking a moment to let the man calm himself again before she spoke, "Well, I am certainly sorry that you had to find out that way. Clearly you were very close. How long had you and Clarissa known each other for, if you don't mind me asking?"

"Since our college days, but then there was a long period of time where I lived abroad, and though we kept in touch with each other sporadically with

Christmas cards and the like, it was only ten years or so ago that we actually met up again."

"So you were at art college too, with Clarissa and Lizzie?"

"I was, though my talent is not in the same league as theirs, nowhere near," Martin blushed and stood up to leave, "Thank you, Flora, I have taken up too much of your time already, I wished only to see where it had happened with my own eyes, then the light from your little house was so welcoming, I..."

Flora turned away as the man reached into his pocket and produced a pristine white cotton handkerchief with which to wipe surreptitiously at his watery eyes. Reggie chose that moment to fly back into the room, squawking "My Flora!" and "Stupid git!" and causing Martin to flinch and duck.

"Reggie! Calm or cage!" Flora shouted, her own nerves feeling frazzled now, and any relaxation the bath had given her totally forgotten, "I'm so sorry, Martin."

"Ah, yes, well," Martin rushed out into the hallway and then out of the front door without turning to face Flora again, his back hunched giving him an air of frailty. Flora felt genuinely sorry for the man, though there was little she could do to help him. After all, they barely knew each other, and then only in a professional capacity. She did hope, though, that he had some friends who could support him through this, as she had the community around her.

With the door safely locked and bolted behind him, Flora turned her attention to the little parrot who was perched on the hallway window sill and looking at her as if butter wouldn't melt, "Well, Reginald Parrot, what do you have to say for yourself?" Flora asked, though gently so she wouldn't startle him.

"My Flora, she's a corker!" Reggie squawked, flying to land on her shoulder, then hopping to the crook in Flora's neck and nuzzling there happily.

"Hmm," Flora said, knowing she couldn't stay angry at the cheeky little chap for long, "I think we need to get back to your training, we clearly still have a long way to go!"

Before she could settle them both in the sitting room to do that very thing, however, the doorbell rang for a second time, "Surely he can't have forgotten anything!" Flora exclaimed to Reggie, as she huffed her way back to the front door. Making a point of taking an extraordinarily long time to unlock the door and finally creak it open just a notch, Flora was shocked to see the unwelcome forms of detectives Blackett and McArthur on the other side, both looking decidedly impatient and displeased.

Clearly, this evening was not going to get any better. Far from it, in fact.

THIRTEEN

Feeling rather underdressed for the occasion in her nightwear, Flora perched uncomfortably on the armchair in her sitting room, whilst the two detectives sat opposite her on the settee, their faces grim. Reggie had been shut in the bedroom after a particularly rude outburst on their arrival where he used some vocabulary inherited from Harold that was certainly not fit for polite ears! Quite shocked, and putting it down to him being unsettled from the events of the weekend, Flora simply told him to be quiet and shut the door. Perhaps she needed to do some more research on how to unlearn learnt behaviour in parrots, but now was not the time. Her mind kept flicking back and forth, however, between images of Reggie alone –

even though he was probably lording it up having a lovely snooze on her pillow – and trying to focus on exactly what the police were saying.

"Mrs. Miller?" McArthur said, looking exasperated.

"Could you repeat the question please?" Flora snapped back, her patience all but spent.

"Please, Mrs. Miller, pay attention," Blackett barked, his thick black eyebrows drawn together in annoyance.

"Really? It must be what? Eight? Eight thirty? On a Sunday evening, when I've, quite frankly, had another weekend from hell, and you're asking me to pay attention?" Flora couldn't quite believe she'd said it, but it was out now and so she sat up straighter and owned her words.

"Well really," Blackett began, an ominous shadow over the grim line of his mouth, until McArthur interrupted him.

"Look, Flora… may I call you that?"

"You may."

"Look, Flora, we none of us hoped to be dealing with each other again so soon – or at all in fact – in another investigation. Yet here we are. We appreciate your frustration as we share it, but we must make our enquiries as soon as possible, strike while the iron's hot and all that."

"I understand," Flora said miserably, "go ahead then."

"Very well," McArthur continued, "can you tell us how the deceased came to be in the village that day?"

Flora began at the beginning, and detailed her numerous attempts at contacting the illustrator, the woman's reputation for scathing reviews, Flora's own desire to have her work on her stories despite bearing the brunt of Clarissa's rudeness herself this past week, as well as her diva demands regarding the opening event. She then explained how Martin was involved as the woman's P.A. and how, from Flora's own point of view, things had unfolded on the actual day of the murder. McArthur took quick notes the whole time, whilst Blackett's stony silence and harsh glare never wavered.

"Thank you, Flora, that is very comprehensive. Now can you tell us about the last time you saw the deceased?"

"Actually, before that," Blackett interrupted rather rudely, "how about you tell us why we saw Martin Loughbrough leaving as we approached."

Flora was shocked by the sudden change in questioning, but was determined not to let that fact show and replied firmly, "Ah, well he called by as he had wanted to see where it had all happened – to Clarissa – and then he knocked on my door. Believe me, I was as surprised as anyone!" Flora hoped his visit didn't raise any suspicion, though why it would she didn't know. Nevertheless, she had to control her anxious hands by grasping them firmly in her lap.

McArthur gave Blackett a look, as if challenging him to interrupt again, and then continued, "Thank you, so about the last time you saw the deceased?"

"Yes, she was storming out of my new bookshop after having upset my friend and her partner, insulted the children present and our village newsletter editor – who is a volunteer himself, I might add. Oh, then I saw her stopping, somewhat reluctantly I imagine, to talk to one of the local schoolteachers. At that point I had to try to rescue the event, so my attention was diverted from the doorway."

"Very well, and the friend you mention, who was upset, that was the Amy you've already mentioned in your description of the day's proceedings, the one who met Ms. Cutter here and then was sick and passed out?" McArthur asked.

"Yes, exactly, and her partner is Gareth Timpson, whom I believe you have already spoken to."

Neither of the detectives either confirmed or denied this, even though their reticence was probably pointless at this stage – the whole village and half of the surrounding area would know by now that Gareth had been taken in for questioning. As a local plumber, his face was recognised by many.

"We will probably have to speak to you again, Flora, but for now could you tell us one last thing?"

"Do I have a choice?"

"Ah, well," McArthur chose to ignore the question, "were you missing anything from either your tearoom or shop after the event?"

"Actually yes, the tailors' shears which we had planned to use to cut the ribbon were missing from behind the counter in the tearoom," Flora spoke clearly and with no hesitancy. She was determined neither to feel nor to show any guilt. That the scissors had been on her property did not mean she was party to murder in any way, shape or form. Nor did she disclose that Adam had shared with her his suspicions that they were indeed the murder weapon, as yet still missing.

"The shears which belong to Mrs. Jean..," McArthur checked her notebook, "Mrs. Jean Sykes who owns the local grocery store?"

"Exactly," Flora let out a long sigh and challenged Blackett with a stare of her own. Part of her wished she had kept Reggie in the room, as she could do with one of his timely interruptions right about now.

It turned out there was no need, however, as McArthur put her notebook and pen back in her pocket and the two stood up to leave.

"We will be in touch when we have more questions," Blackett said, "but in the meantime I do expect you to call us if you hear anything, Mrs. Miller, and don't even think about doing one of your own little investigations! Strange how you always manage to find the culprits in these local cases, is it not?"

"It is rather, considering you're the ones being paid to find them!" Flora bit back, and was secretly proud of herself for her quick-witted retort. Perhaps some of Reggie's feistiness was beginning to rub off on her, she thought.

Blackett's eyebrows shot up into his forehead at Flora's perceived impertinence, but he held his tongue as the two detectives made their way out. Flora leant back against the strong wooden door after their departure and took several deep breaths, before making sure it was all locked up yet again and then hurrying to the bedroom to release her reluctant captive.

"Sad! Sad! Bad bird! Bad bird!" Reggie screeched, taking off from where he had been dozing on the bed, and swooping for the door the moment he realised his imprisonment was over. The words cut through Flora and tugged on her heartstrings, so that she rushed with the small bird on her shoulder into the kitchen and immediately produced two more juicy, round grapes from the fridge both to placate and to apologise.

"Not again! Not again!" Reggie squawked after making swift work of the treat, and Flora slumped back down in her armchair sharing Reggie's sentiment, the events of recent days taking their toll. Tomorrow would mark the start of a new week, and Flora dearly hoped it would be better than the last.

FOURTEEN

Determined to stick to the normal routine that Monday morning – despite a thumping headache, and a parrot who was still sulking from the night before – Flora dragged herself along to the tearoom by the new roundabout route she and Adam had found. It took a few minutes longer, and left Flora with several mud stains on her tweed trousers, but she was at least there by opening time. Having assumed that Mondays would probably be quiet in both the tearoom and bookshop, Tanya's new part time hours began on Tuesday each week, meaning that Flora would be alone juggling both sides of her little enterprise today. As she laid the vintage crockery out on the tables, Flora dearly hoped that the day would prove to be quiet and uneventful, and thus provide a chance to get her mind back in order.

When the bell above the tearoom door tinkled one minute after opening, Flora was therefore somewhat disgruntled. She nipped back through from where she had been checking that everything in the bookshop had been tidied up from Saturday's non-event and was relieved to see that it was Amy and not a gaggle of hikers hoping for bacon buns before they set out on one of the many local routes.

"Amy! Come in, how are you?"

"So-so, this sickness bug or whatever I've got hasn't gone away," Amy said, "but I'm due in the salon for ten, and I hoped to have a quick word with you Flora, if that's okay?"

"Of course! Tea?"

"Yes please, hello Reggie," Amy came to sit at the table nearest the counter and smiled at the little bird who was perched on the handle of her empty teacup.

"Reggie, manners!" Flora chided, but the parrot's selective hearing kicked in and he didn't budge at all.

"So," Flora began when they were both sitting with a cup of Earl Grey and a scone each, "how have things been? How's Gareth?"

"Well, he's exactly the reason I've come, actually," Amy said quietly. She paused, as if wondering whether she should go on, and Flora waited patiently. At length, the young woman seemed to come to a decision, "Flora, do you think he could have done it? The murder, I mean, I've never seen him that angry. The police came to interview me yesterday afternoon, and I admitted as much to them, and now I'm worried I dropped Gareth in it!"

Amy's chin wobbled, and Flora could tell she was getting upset. Reaching out to stroke her friend's arm, Flora reassured her, "No, Amy, from what you've told me before of Gareth, and from how I've seen him treat Lewis, I don't think he would kill someone and risk being put in prison away from his son. You have only told the police the truth so have nothing to feel guilty about. That being said, I would be lying if I said things are looking good for Gareth. I imagine he might be the detectives' top suspect right now. I know how that feels, and I'd not be surprised if Gareth is a bit distant at the moment."

"Well, he was acting strangely with me before this, so I can only imagine how distant he'll be now," Amy began weeping softly.

"Hopefully a resolution to the investigation will be quick in coming, then," Flora said gently, and Amy nodded. Seeing the young woman upset, Reggie jumped onto her arm and nuzzled his head into her sleeve, eliciting a watery smile from Amy.

"Gareth said that he didn't storm off after Ms. Cutter that day, he insists that he went in the other direction, up to the manor house, for a walk around the grounds to calm down."

"And do you have any reason not to believe him?" Flora asked.

"I don't think so – I don't know, I'm so confused Flora. I love him, but even before this I got the impression maybe he's gone off me. Perhaps he was trying to find the right way to let me down gently?" Amy was crying in earnest now, and Flora stood and put her arm around her.

"Oh Amy, relationships can be so complicated. It's a wonder any of them survive!"

"I know, I was just wondering," Amy wiped her nose on the very expensive tissue Flora offered her – straight from the box which had been brought in at Clarissa Cutter's specific request, "I was wondering if you could talk to him, Flora?"

"Me? Talk to Gareth?" Flora squeaked, "Oh Amy, I barely know the man..."

"Yes, but you're so good with people. You could maybe ask him to do some plumbing work and then chat to him, and it wouldn't seem like a deliberate inquisition?"

"Well, I," Flora looked at Amy's tear-stained face and the little bird who was still on her arm with his head cocked to one side, his perceptive little eyes seemingly assessing his owner, and in a moment of weakness – of madness, she would later call it – Flora agreed, "Okay then, I'll see if he can fit in a quick visit. The toilet up here does seem to have a small problem with the flush. I'm not promising anything, mind."

"Thank you so much, Flora!" Amy stood up and gave Flora a huge hug. Flora patted her back absentmindedly, already regretting her decision.

After a flying visit from Lily with some cakes from the farm shop and an invite for Flora to come up for dinner later in the week, plus several texts from Adam asking how she was, Flora finally plucked up the courage to text Gareth on the number Amy had given her before she left. In a rather brief, but surprisingly easy message thread, Flora arranged for the man in question to come and look at the bathroom in the tearoom the next morning, if he finished the installation he was currently working on in Witherington. Flora's gut seemed to have an instinctive reaction since she came to the village – perhaps it was all the investigations she had been privy to – but it never failed to let her know when something felt wrong. And this felt wrong. Flora knew that, at the very least, she shouldn't be getting involved in the case, and trying to get information out of the prime suspect definitely fell under that umbrella. In a spur of the moment decision, Flora decided not to tell Adam about it at all. She would keep her promise to Amy, and then bury the matter in her own mind without discussing it with anyone else.

As Flora ruminated on this, the door to the tearoom flew open and the Marshall girls arrived with Sally, the older two still in their school uniforms, and with so much energy it was like they hadn't been to school at all.

"Sorry," Sally apologised before the group had even sat down, "we're all full of beans today!"

"You know I love it when the place comes to life," Flora reassured her, though her attention was on the window, where Flora had spotted an old car chugging into the driveway outside.

"Welcome to the tearoom!" Reggie squawked, happy to see the girls, who had swiftly become his favourite visitors. The children discarded their coats where they fell and rushed straight through to the bookshop to browse.

"Don't make any mess! And only get one book off the shelf at a time!" Sally warned, letting out a small sigh.

The bell above the door tinkled and Martin Loughbrough arrived, looking much more his usual put-together self than he had the previous evening. Flora was shocked to see the man again so soon, and simply greeted him briefly before going to take Sally's order and then disappearing behind the counter. As much as she sympathised with the poor man, Flora didn't want to be seen to be forming any kind of bond with him, not while the police were poking around. Also, she had enough on her plate without becoming his emotional crutch. Flora felt guilty and harsh even as the thought passed through her mind, but she couldn't help it.

A resounding shriek of "Not that jerk!" brought Flora back to the present, where Reggie had clearly come back through from the bookshop – where he had been basking in the girls' attention – and noticed the new arrival. Flora scanned the room, grateful that the youngsters were not there and must still be looking at the books. Hopefully they hadn't heard her pet's coarse language.

"I'm so sorry," Flora apologised to both Martin and Sally for the bird's outburst, and quickly scooped him up from where he had landed on Martin's table, bringing him behind the counter with her.

"Bad bird!" Flora tutted and tapped his beak, whilst simultaneously feeling sorry for her little friend. His life had been very unsettled for the past few months, since Flora had inherited him in fact, and she decided then and there that once this investigation was over, she would take a break to focus on the bird. He was her family now, and therefore a priority.

Heaven knows, Flora thought to herself, *I could do with some time off myself!*

FIFTEEN

Flora's phone buzzed as she was preparing a pot of tea for she and Sally to share and a cappuccino for Martin. What the man wanted now, Flora had no idea, nor did she really have the inclination to find out. The message was from Lizzie, inviting Flora over for an evening meal the next day. Flora thought back to the chaos of her opening event on Saturday, and struggled to recall when Lizzie had left – had Flora even said goodbye to the artist? Feeling embarrassed and that she may have inadvertently been rude, Flora replied that she would love to. It would mean a drive to Alnwick in the dark, and Flora hoped the roads wouldn't be wet or icy, but perhaps it would do her good to get out of the village for a few hours.

Text sent, and Reggie having some time out on the

naughty perch, Flora served Martin his drink and made a point of being friendly but cool. She certainly didn't want to encourage the man by seeming to welcome his new daily visits.

"Would you like to join me?" Martin asked politely, though eying the large teapot Flora also carried on her tray.

"No, thank you for the offer Martin, but Sally and I have much to discuss about the relocation of the Knit and Natter club to the bookshop from the church hall."

"Oh well, don't let me keep you from important village business," Martin smiled and gave a half-laugh, and Flora felt guilty for being icy with him as she took a seat opposite Sally.

Flora told the vicar's wife in hushed tones about her visit from the two detectives the previous evening, and then they spoke about Amy – though Flora didn't mention Amy's request that she speak to Gareth – and the implications for the village from being under the scrutiny of another murder investigation. Sally said that her husband, James, had been under pressure from the Bishop to bring a sense of peace and tranquillity back to the residents of the village and that, as yet, he had not thought of any good ways to do so. Apparently, the ladies of the W.I. were having some sort of internal unrest – which Flora had already heard a little of from Betty – and this was causing problems with the scheduling for the weekly Senior Lunches and Classic Film Club which they normally organised in the village hall.

"Surely, the internal workings of that institution can't be James' responsibility?" Flora asked, genuinely intrigued.

"No, not really, but the contentment of the parishioners is, and the Bishop has already received one or two communications from older folk in the area who feel their usual, and relied upon, social interactions have been disturbed by the in-fighting," Sally sighed and poured them each another cup. The girls were being worryingly quiet, and she took a moment to poke her head around the opening in the wall connecting them with the bookshop.

"Are they okay?" Flora whispered.

"Yes, little Megan has fallen asleep on the beanbags and the older two are drawing. They must've finally used up all their energy!"

"Indeed…" Flora was interrupted by Martin, who had finished his cappuccino, and was standing with his overcoat hanging on his arm, not showing any signs of putting it on. His three-piece suit and matching silk cravat looked pristine and his shoes well-polished since the evening before when Flora recalled they had been splattered with mud.

"Do you mind if I have a look at the books?" Martin asked, hovering in the gap between the two spaces.

"Not at all," Flora replied, though she waited until he had gone through to suggest to Sally that they also take their cups of tea and go through to the bookshop, to keep an eye on the girls.

"Absolutely," Sally whispered back, "I was a schoolteacher before I married, and it would never do to leave a strange adult with the children. It's made me a very cautious parent."

"Sensible in my book," Flora said, as they both took a seat on the small sofa from where they could watch the girls drawing.

Martin looked at the non-fiction books in the historical section for a while, before meandering over to the two women, just as Evie came over with her latest masterpiece.

"Well, that is special," Martin said, seemingly genuinely interested in the drawing. He spoke to Evie about her picture for a minute or so and then the little girl asked him if he could show her how to draw a dragon.

Martin hesitated and looked to Flora and Sally for an answer.

"Of course," Sally said, "as long as Mr…"

"Loughbrough"

"As long as Mr. Loughbrough doesn't mind."

"It would be my pleasure," Martin said, taking the stool which belonged behind the small bookshop counter and positioning it beside the child-size chairs which the girls were using. Sally and Flora watched for a bit and then, as Martin and the girls were focused on their art, the women began to chat again in hushed tones.

About half an hour had gone by, and Flora was just beginning to think she should be clearing up for the evening, when the door to the tearoom burst open and Tanya flew in. The woman's red hair had been transformed to a new platinum blonde colour, and she was wearing a fleecy jumpsuit that looked rather like Tigger from the Winnie the Pooh books, complete with ears and tail. Flora wondered if her friend had been on some acting gig but didn't like to ask – after all, the outfit must surely be cosy and warm which was the main consideration here in Northumberland in the winter.

"Flora!" Tanya was struggling to catch her breath. Her cheeks were ruddy and her eyes sparkled as if she had been running.

Flora jumped up, suddenly panicked herself that something might be majorly wrong, "Tanya! What is it?"

Sally came straight over to join them as well, though Martin stayed with the girls, distracting them from the sudden arrival.

"She's a corker!" Reggie screeched on seeing Tanya, but didn't receive his usual reply, which further worried Flora.

"Tanya, what is it? What's happened?" Flora asked, feeling the anxiety pressing on her chest.

"My Pat," she coughed.

"Pat? Is he okay?" Sally asked.

"Yes, my Pat, he was doing his rounds of the village, walked all the way up the lane past the turnoff to here," Tanya paused to catch her breath, "with Frank, then the dog got the scent for something. You remember he was a famous police dog before retiring here to work with my Pat?"

"Yes, yes," Flora was getting impatient, and it was starting to show.

"Well, Frank got the scent and he was off! My Pat ran to catch up and the dog was in the bushes, the ones that run at the back of your coach house, Flora, and along the main road. Well, guess what? He only went and found the murder weapon! My Pat! Well, it was Frank really, and we don't know for sure it was the murder weapon, but still! The murderer must've panicked and thrown it under there. The detectives are at my house now and I came straight here to tell you!" Tanya was gulping in the air she needed and Flora indicated that she should take a seat.

"I think this calls for more tea!" Flora said.

"Of course, the detectives said I shouldn't give out information about the weapon itself, so my lips are sealed on that," Tanya said ruefully, and Flora could almost see the struggle it took her friend not to blurt out all she knew.

"Mummy look at our pictures! Look at what the kind

man drawed for us!" the girls interrupted them at an opportune moment, saving Tanya from the pain of not being able to elaborate further. Little Megan rubbed her sleepy eyes and climbed onto Sally's lap.

"Drew dear, he drew them," Sally corrected gently, "well, aren't these magnificent!"

It was only then, as they looked back into the bookshop to praise Martin for his work, that the women realised he was gone.

"Strange man," Sally said, though they had much more important things to talk about, and the three women chatted about what this new development could mean for the investigation, all hoping that it would aid in a swift cracking of the case. As the girls became more tired and darkness had long since fallen outside, Sally and Tanya left to walk back to the village together, holding hands with the three little ones. Flora tidied and cleaned up in the tearoom before moving to the bookshop to put the pencils and crayons back in their baskets. The Marshall girls had taken their favourite drawings and left the rest – in a higgledy-piggledy mess on the table – muddled together with some beautiful illustrations which must have come from Martin. Considering them too lovely to simply throw away, Flora decided to order a cork board online on which she could pin up any future creations, and so slipped the drawings into the drawer behind the counter for now.

It was an exhausted Flora and a grumpy little bird who made their way along the circuitous route to the coach house. Flora couldn't help herself – she deliberately took an even longer detour so that she could see exactly where the weapon had been found. She was in no doubt in her own mind that it must be Jean's tailoring shears, but had known better than to mention this to Tanya and Sally. The thick bushes to the side of the lane had been cordoned off and Flora could see a flashlight or two shining further back within the branches.

Flora gave a shiver which had little to do with the chill February evening and more to do with the thought of what the shears had been used for. She pulled her scarf closer around her neck, and suddenly regretted coming this way by herself. She really needed to stop adding to her list of bad decisions, Flora decided, picking up her pace and chatting to Reggie as she walked, giving herself the illusion that she was not so alone.

SIXTEEN

Flora ate a plain supper of scrambled eggs on toast, her stomach feeling too tied up in knots to try anything else. Then she chatted to Adam on the phone, hoping that he would help her general malaise. Unfortunately, their conversation turned almost immediately to the investigation, not helping Flora's worries. Whilst he didn't explicitly say it was Jean's scissors which had been found, Adam's carefully chosen words did lead Flora to believe that she had been correct in her assumption. She spoke to him about her conversations with both Martin, and Blackett and McArthur the night before, as well as about Martin's appearance at the tearoom again that day.

"Why do you think he keeps showing up here?" Flora asked, genuinely curious.

"Well, he could be missing her, he'd been working for Clarissa for a decade, hadn't he? And they'd known each other a lot longer," Adam suggested, "so it could be that he suddenly has a lot of free time on his hands and is feeling a bit lost. Alternatively, he could be keen to see where it happened and to follow the investigation, wanting to make sure she gets the justice she deserves. Or maybe he did it, and it's important to find out what the police know. Who knows?"

"Goodness, yes, that's a lot of possibilities," Flora sighed, "From the totally innocent to the positively guilty!"

"Quite, that's why it's so important that you don't get involved – with discussing the case with him or anyone else whom the police are interested in," Adam said, "promise me you'll leave well alone."

It was as if he could read her mind, and for a moment Flora was silent, "Of course, of course," she replied. She hadn't planned to tell Adam about her appointment with Gareth tomorrow, and now she was certainly not going to. In fact, the closer it got, the more Flora knew she had done the wrong thing. She considered texting Gareth to cancel.

"Flora, love, you okay? I'm at work, but I can call by if you're freaked out about everything?" Adam had obviously picked up on her sudden silence.

"No, no I'm fine, it's just been another long day is all."

"Well, no more thinking about the murder case, okay? Let the detectives do their job – you never know, you might find we're quite good at it!" Adam joked, but Flora could barely bring herself to smile. She ended the call quickly and decided to forgo her usual bath in favour of an early night. There was too much going around in her head, and Flora wanted to rush headlong into the relative calm of sleep.

Calm was the furthest from how Flora felt when she was rather rudely awoken about two hours earlier than usual the next morning. Reggie was doing flying loops of the small hallway, screeching randomly and only occasionally peppering his loud outburst with actual words, "Somebody else! Visitors!" and the like. Flora wasn't sure what had got into him, but was determined to eke out her sleep for as long as possible so tried telling him to be quiet from the bed. This had no effect other than to cause Reggie to pause very briefly in his explosion of feathers and sound, and Flora was finally able to hear what must've woken the bird and started him off in the first place. A large fuss was coming from outside the front of the coach house, on Flora's gravel driveway by the sounds of it, so Flora reluctantly got out of bed and pulled her robe around her to investigate.

Peering out of the hallway window, and craning her neck, Flora managed to catch sight of a large, white van adorned with numerous aerials, and a whole news crew busy setting up cameras.

"What the?" Flora asked, unlocking the door and flinging it wide, not caring that she was still in her nightwear. It seemed so many people had seen her in less than ideal states of dress in recent months, that Flora barely cared any longer.

"What are you doing?" she asked, though in truth it was quite obvious what the visitors were doing.

"Just getting set up," a beefy man in tracksuit bottoms and a hoodie shouted back without looking up from the camera he was carrying.

"I can see that," Flora's hands went to her hips, "What I mean is, why are you doing it on private land, my land?"

"Ah you must be Mrs. Baker," a petite woman with bright blonde hair and fuchsia lipstick came almost skipping over, her bubbliness more than Flora could take at this time of day.

"Ms. Miller, the village is Baker's Rise," Flora said slowly, as if talking to a child.

"Yes, well, we just heard about another recent murder here, details are still sketchy, but the boss wants it on the breakfast news…" she was interrupted by another van pulling up, with 'Daily Courier' emblazoned on the side. This then jostled for a parking place with an Alnwick Airwaves radio station car which was not more than two seconds behind it.

"Not more," Flora lamented, before turning her attention back to the woman, "well, this is private land, and are you even sure the police want you to be walking all over their investigation? Do you have their permission to be here?"

The woman simply shrugged her shoulders and plastered on her fake smile, "We'll be going live in ten minutes, so if you don't want to be interviewed in your pyjamas, I suggest you get a hurry on," she said, a small part of her true character coming through in the rather smug way the news presenter said it.

Knowing what Adam would have to say about her giving an interview caused Flora to pause and consider. Then again, she thought, if not me then they'll just find someone like Edwina Edwards to speak to them instead. Someone who won't hesitate to speak their mind. Seeing it as the lesser of two evils, Flora therefore decided to quickly get dressed in one of her city suits and rushed back out of the door, leaving Reggie in the cottage.

The bushes and plants lining the small driveway were laden with frost, and Flora shivered as she patted down her hair. She had barely had time to brush it let alone style it in any way, and hoped it would look neat enough on camera. By the time the producer gestured for Flora to come over for her interview, Daisy Doxford had already done a small, live piece to camera, whilst the journalist from a local paper had taken rapid notes.

Suddenly all eyes were on Flora, her mouth went dry and her mind blank as soon as the link to the television studio went live.

"So, Ms. Miller, is it true that the deceased was at an event at your new bookshop shortly before she died?" Daisy asked nonchalantly.

"Well, I mean, she had been booked to appear, but then she barely got to the front door before the arguing started, so she didn't really attend the event at all," Flora's cheeks flushed red as she stuttered over the words.

The interviewer's eyes glinted as she latched onto what Flora had indiscreetly let slip, "The arguing? And what arguing would that be then?"

"Well, I mean, there wasn't really, I mean," Flora couldn't seem to think straight let alone get her words in order. The only thought that chimed in her head was that she had already said too much, far too much. But the interview was live, so she had to say something, and fast, "Well, ah, a local lady who was helping me with the event had borne the brunt of Ms. Cutter's, ah the deceased's, bad temper earlier in the morning," as soon as the words were out, Flora regretted them, as now the press would want to sniff out who that was, and if they found out it was sweet, shy Amy then the poor young woman would be suffocated under their onslaught. Panic began to build in Flora's stomach and rise to her chest.

"Ms. Baker, I was asking whom this was, this local lady," Daisy persevered, clearly trying to mask her exasperation at the fact Flora kept tuning her out.

"Oh, well, I had a lot of people helping me on the day," Flora desperately tried to backtrack. She was aware that she was no doubt sounding flaky and forgetful, and hardly painting her little tearoom and bookshop in a good light.

"Indeed," the woman pressed on with a few more questions in a similar vein but, realising she was getting nowhere, suddenly changed tack, "and we have reason to believe that, not only were you yourself a murder suspect just a couple of short months ago, but you are also dating one of the detectives who investigated the murder of Harold Baker, your predecessor as owner of this estate. Can you confirm that?"

That was it, that was her coup de grâce, and she knew it. Her bright lips turned up warmly at the corners, though her eyes had an animalistic coldness about them as the presenter directed her unwavering gaze at Flora.

Flora didn't want to lie, but neither did she want to discuss her personal life with the whole of the northeast news viewing population. Drawing herself up to her full height, and only then realising that she had given the whole interview in her fluffy house slippers, Flora looked Miss Daisy Doxford straight in the eye and said, "This village has certainly been at the centre of some very upsetting and disturbing events in recent months, which is all the more reason why we value our privacy at this time."

Finally, she had managed to say something vaguely

correct, but Flora was very well aware that it was most likely a case of much too little, much too late. The whole interview had been a shambles, from her point of view anyway – she had clearly given the press some great leads to follow and was thanked heartily by the guy from the Courier, who sauntered back to his van with a grin on his face as if he were the cat that had just got the cream.

Flora's own legs felt like jelly, and as the team dismantled the set almost as fast as they had built it, she let herself back into the coach house wearily. There was not enough sweet tea or caffeinated beverages in the world to sustain her through the rest of today, Flora thought miserably, especially considering the number of villagers who would surely find time to 'pop in' to the tearoom for a chat once they had seen the local news broadcast. No, Flora wanted nothing better than to go back to bed and hide under her duvet.

Sadly, life had other ideas, as her phone was already ringing when Flora entered the house.

SEVENTEEN

"Flora, goodness me lass, are you okay? That was quite an interview – no Harry, I tell you she will want to be talking to me – don't you Flora?"

"Hello Betty, yes, it was rather an impromptu, spur of the moment thing."

"Yes, well I think we could all tell that, truth be told," Betty was nothing if not honest, and Flora sank down onto her armchair, Reggie peering at her curiously and for once staying sensibly silent.

"I'm regretting it already actually," Flora said, feeling thoroughly sorry for herself. She accepted Reggie's tentative head rubs gratefully against her palm and wished she could start the whole day over again.

"Well, there's no use crying over spilt milk," Betty declared, "what's done is done. If you hadn't made the village famous before with all these investigations, you have now! Anyway, I've need of a space to hold a small meeting with a few select ladies from the W.I. this afternoon – all on the hush hush you understand – and I was wondering if we could use the bookshop?"

"Yes, I don't see why not," Flora knew resistance was futile at the best of times, and right now she had no energy to try to deflect Betty's plan. Once the older woman had an idea in her head there was very little that could deter her.

"Betty, let the lass be getting ready for work!" Flora could hear Harry in the background, and was grateful when it led to Betty cutting the conversation short. Well, thankful until her phone began ringing again as soon as that call had ended.

"Hello," Flora saw Adam's number flash up on the screen and did her best to sound chirpy.

"Flora, what were you, I mean, I don't want to sound, it's just I… sorry love, what was that interview all about? Blackett's just about blown a fuse over here in the station."

"I, well, they didn't give me much choice, I woke up to

them all set up outside and…"

"You should've called Pat Hughes, or me, or locked the door and ignored them… or anything but that interview. Flora, they'll be like dogs with a bone now," Adam sighed and Flora felt like a chastised child, "what did I say about keeping a low profile and not getting involved in the investigation?"

Adam's tone was soft but she knew he was angry with her, or frustrated at least, "Well, I guess the damage is done so there's no point in discussing it," Flora said, "I'm running late, I'll speak to you later," and she hung up.

Her breath coming in gasps which heralded the swift arrival of the tears which followed, Flora put the phone down none too gently and dropped her head into her hands. She studiously ignored the ringing as Adam tried to get hold of her again, and simply slumped down, defeated and deflated.

"My Flora, My Flora," the little bird on her knee chirped, as Flora's salty tears rained down on him.

It had taken Flora a while to pull herself back together, to take the shower she had missed and put on some makeup to try to hide her blotchy eyes and face. So, she was running late and arrived at the tearoom to find Gareth already on the doorstep.

"Gareth?" Flora said, before it came flooding back, the whole promise to Amy and the reason why she had texted the plumber in the first place.

"Yes, you asked me to call about the flush on the toilet? I thought I'd pop in on my way to a bigger job in Alnwick."

"Yes, yes, thank you so much for fitting me in, it's just a small thing really, just seems to take a long time to actually flush and then an even longer time refilling afterwards," Flora tried to make the tiny issue which she had barely noticed into something worthy of a call out from a plumber.

"No worries, is it just the little bathroom here in the shop?"

"Yes, just this one, thanks," Flora replied as she grabbed the baked goods from the side of the building and unlocked the door to let them both in. Tanya wasn't due in until ten, so Flora knew that gave her some time alone with Gareth to try to probe him subtly about his feelings for Amy and his whereabouts at the time of the murder. When she thought about it like that, this whole plan seemed even more absurd to Flora, but she was committed now and had to go through with it – to some degree at least – to try to give Amy some peace of mind.

"So, Gareth," Flora began tentatively as the man was kneeling down and bent over in the tiny bathroom, with Flora hovering behind. He was probably wondering why she didn't get on with preparing the tearoom for the day, and Flora herself felt ridiculous standing behind him in that position. It didn't help that Reggie, who had had his feathers ruffled quite enough for one day already with the disturbance from the reporters and then Flora's misery which had worried him no end, began shrieking "Ooh sexy beast!" at that most inopportune moment.

Gareth straightened up quickly and turned his head to look at Flora, his face a deep shade of crimson.

"Fancy a coffee to get you started for the day? And a bacon sandwich?" Flora asked, assuming an air of nonchalance which she did not feel.

"Oh, aye, that would be grand," Gareth said, turning back to his work.

Flora had barely had time to fire up the coffee machine and put the bacon in the pan on the hob when Gareth was already finished, and standing beside the counter.

"That's all sorted, Flora, just needed a quick tightening up," he said, looking slightly perplexed.

"Excellent, excellent, how much do I owe you, for the call out and everything?"

"Oh, nothing, really, this breakfast more than covers it, really there wasn't much of a problem to solve to be honest."

The bacon was sizzling and Flora added the coffee to the machine. It was now or never if she was going to question Gareth, "So, um, I'm really sorry about Saturday. If I'd known you had a personal connection with… well, I never would have asked you and Amy to go up to the coach house to meet her."

"Aye well, you weren't to know, I don't talk about my late wife all that much, even less so the people who made her short life miserable," Gareth's face was turning puce and Flora could feel the anger coming off him in waves.

Nevertheless, like the silly woman she was, she persevered, "And afterwards, when she had stormed out and you followed after her, you…?" Flora left the question hanging. *Very subtle, Flora,* she thought to herself, *subtle as a sledgehammer*.

Gareth's eyes narrowed and his nostrils flared whilst he seemed to be judging his next response carefully, "Did Amy put you up to this? She's been fretting over where I was and what I did next."

"What? Of course not!" Flora turned her back on him quickly to attend to the bacon and butter the bread bun.

"Good, she's getting herself far too worked up, I'm worried about her to be honest. If you do see her, please try to put her mind at ease, will you Flora?"

"Of course, of course I will," Flora handed him the sandwich wrapped in a paper bag and put the finishing touches to the coffee in a take-out cardboard cup.

"I think I've been a bit… a bit off with her lately, even before all this happened, and I hadn't meant to be, it's just…"

"Yes?" Flora encouraged the man, though she felt guilty that she had trapped him into this conversation and now here he was opening up to her.

"Well, as you now know I was married before, and it can be hard… when you've lost someone you loved that dearly… to realise – a good while later though – that you love someone else just as much and want to spend the rest of your life with them. It can be… scary, and it takes a good deal of soul searching to not feel guilty towards the person you've lost. To not feel like you're betraying them and what you had."

"I can imagine," Flora said gently, understanding now that what Amy had seen as Gareth putting a worrying distance between the couple, had actually been him coming to terms with his strong feelings for her so that he could find peace with the situation.

"I'm so sorry, Flora," Gareth shook his head ruefully, I shouldn't have offloaded all that on you. I'm just short on people to confide in, I guess."

"Not at all, and for what it's worth, I think it's always a good idea to pause every now and then and re-evaluate, to take stock of how we feel. It'll make for a much stronger relationship between you and Amy in the future if you make peace with your past now."

"Thank you, Flora, you're right," Gareth smiled, and Flora really felt sympathy for the man. He must be what thirty? Thirty two? And he had already been through so much.

"Morning Flora, oh hello Gareth!" Tanya waltzed into

the tearoom with her usual dramatic entrance and brought a halt to their conversation. Blushing again, Gareth thanked Flora quickly for the food, grabbed his workbag and rushed out.

"She's a corker!" Reggie squawked, though didn't leave the comfort of his perch, where he had been snoozing off his morning's stresses.

"Well, you've had quite the day already!" Tanya winked and at first Flora thought she was making some lewd reference to Gareth being there, and then she remembered. Obviously she had managed to blank this morning's interview out of her mind and now it all came flooding back, in all its technicolour glory.

"Oh Tanya," Flora said miserably, "what have I done?"

EIGHTEEN

Once she had shared a pot of Earl Grey with Tanya, and they had narrowed down that Flora had really only told the press two things: that there had been an argument and that before that Clarissa Cutter had upset someone, it didn't seem quite as bad. Clarissa's temper was well known already and, unless someone else in the village gave them the exact details, all the reporters had were some general leads. So Flora kept telling herself, on repeat, the whole morning. The tearoom and bookshop had a steady stream of local customers to keep both she and Tanya busy, so it wasn't until after lunchtime that Flora was finally able to sit down again. Not that she minded, as keeping busy meant she had less time to contemplate.

When the bell above the door tinkled just before two

o'clock and a line of half a dozen ladies from the local Women's Institute trailed in after Betty, the whole group of them looking somewhat shifty, Flora was reminded of her promise to Betty that morning.

"Betty, ladies, welcome. I know you wanted the bookshop, but since the tearoom is also empty, wouldn't you be more comfortable in here?"

"No lass!" Betty replied quickly, "This is not a regular meeting if you understand my drift," Betty winked twice and led the group into the bookshop.

Flora wasn't sure she did get her drift, but simply shrugged her shoulders realising with interest that Edwina Edwards, as Chairwoman of the local group, was notably absent. Tanya helped to furnish the ladies with enough chairs from the tearoom for them to sit comfortably in a circle, and cups of tea and slices of cake were similarly carried through.

"A lot of bother, when they could just sit in the tearoom!" Tanya said to Flora in a stage whisper, and Flora had to agree. Tanya's shift finished at two, so she said her goodbyes and then disappeared, leaving Flora twiddling her thumbs in the empty tearoom and trying desperately not to eavesdrop on the hushed conversation coming from the other room.

A car pulling up outside distracted both she and Reggie from the whispers, and the small bird flew straight to the window sill, so they both peered out. Where normally she would feel a flutter of happiness at Adam's arrival, today Flora was assailed with a sinking dread.

"Secrets and Lies!" Reggie squawked and Flora couldn't tell whether he was referring to the hushed conversation between the ladies, or to the new arrival, as either could have been true. This saddened Flora, as she had not had secrets from Adam, nor lied to him until now. It was not a precedent she wanted to set in their relationship, and in that second Flora decided it would be best to come clean about her conversation with Gareth and how she had tried to fish for information pertaining to the murder enquiry.

"Hello love," Adam said kissing Flora softly, his normal good humour seemingly restored after their troublesome morning call.

"Hi," she whispered, wanting nothing more than to fling her arms around him and have a good cry. Flora did neither, however, and simply said, "Coffee?"

"Sounds lovely."

Neither of them spoke about the elephant in the room,

and instead they made chitchat, Adam raising his eyebrows at the secret meeting in the other room and causing Flora to giggle. It wasn't until they were sitting at the table closest to the counter, and farthest from the bookshop, that their real conversation began.

"Look, Flora, love I'm sorry about this morning. I was just... surprised. Shocked, I guess, to see you on the television when I was finishing my shift."

"I know, and you have no idea how much I regret it all," Flora said honestly, "If I could go back and just slam the door in her smug face I would, believe me."

"Aye well, you said nothing someone else in the village wouldn't have told them anyway. People are always keen to get their five minutes of fame, even if it is to do with something as grisly as murder."

"Thanks, but I think I'll regret that interview for a long time to come. Anyway, lesson learned, I'm glad you've come, I wanted to tell you something else actually," Flora felt her heart beating rapidly in her chest as she explained Amy's request and her own conversation with Gareth that morning.

"Oh Flora," Adam put his cup down on the saucer slowly and exhaled a deep sigh. Flora began to feel niggled at the thought of him scolding her again, and her hackles began to rise.

"I know what you're going to say, so you might as well not bother!" she said defensively.

"Well, why did you tell me then?" Adam snapped, "Just so I would know you'd broken your promise to me? That you can't help yourself but interfere in other people's lives and in a police investigation? This is serious business, Flora!"

"I'm well aware of that! A friend asked me to help!" Flora bit back, and then they both stared at each other, both biting their tongue and having reached an impasse. That their whole argument was being held in whispers so the elderly women next door couldn't hear, would have struck Flora as humorous at any other time, but right now she just felt sick. This was her first proper argument with Adam, and whilst she knew it was healthy to disagree in a relationship, Flora simply felt like a child who was being told off yet again.

"You must understand," Adam said eventually, covering Flora's hand gently with his own, "that it reflects badly on me at work, with the other detectives, when you keep sticking your nose into our investigations. I've told Blackett and McArthur you won't interfere again – because you'd given me your word that you wouldn't – and yet, here you are, telling me that's exactly what you've done!" He sounded exasperated, and disappointed, and Flora couldn't bear it any longer. She pulled her hand out with much more force than was necessary, and stood up abruptly, just as all the ladies began to file out behind Betty.

"Thank you, Flora," Betty said with a regal head tilt as she left, looking particularly pleased with herself.

As each woman walked past Reggie's perch he squawked, "Visitors! Visitors with money!" as if he were begging on the streets of a large city, and not sitting plumped up and well fed in a beautiful vintage tearoom.

"Reggie!" Flora said in her warning voice, earning her a flash of a wing and a piercing glance, before he changed tack and the silly bird screeched, "You old trout!" startling poor Mrs. May who nearly tripped over her own walking stick.

"I'm so sorry," Flora was mortified as she helped the woman regain her balance.

"I'd better be going too," Adam said, and before Flora could reply, he joined the group of dispersing ladies and was at his car before Flora thought to call him back.

"Well, that was rude! Bad bird! Bad Bird! Reginald Parrot you are in disgrace!" Flora said harshly, before she realised she was likely taking out most of her own anger on the bird when she should really be directing it at herself.

Flora was really cross with herself for how she had handled things with Adam and how they had left it with nothing resolved. After all, Flora thought sadly, she had broken a promise, she had lied, and now presumably he might want nothing more to do with her. The thought that her relationship with the gorgeous Detective Bramble might be over brought sudden tears to Flora's eyes and an empty ache in her chest. She had never thought to get into a serious relationship so soon after her divorce, but it had happened, and now Flora wasn't sure she wanted to lose it. *No*, she thought, *I can at least be honest with myself. I don't want to lose it, to lose him*. But Flora wasn't sure what to do about it. For now, she had her meal in Alnwick with Lizzie to get changed for and a bookshop full of teacups to clear away and wash, so Flora put her head down and concentrated on her tasks, ignoring the sulking bird on his perch, who no doubt felt as wretched as she did.

NINETEEN

The drive to Alnwick later that day soothed Flora's soul somewhat and she enjoyed watching the winter sun set below the horizon across the country lanes and fields. She had left Reggie at home, thinking some quiet time apart might do them both good. Flora mostly drove by memory to the studio which she had visited once before when Lizzie had taken the original photos for Reggie's portrait, only needing to consult her Satnav at the end of the journey, as the twisting rural roads were difficult to distinguish from one another.

"Flora, so lovely to see you!" Lizzie greeted Flora at the door and this time they walked straight through the airy studio space and into the cottage which was attached.

"And you, I'm so sorry I didn't get to say goodbye on Saturday, there was just… so much chaos and I had my hands full trying to get everything back on track! It was remiss of me to not see you leave."

"Not at all, it was lovely to see your new place so busy, but I just saw on the news about Clarissa! How awful! As much as I disliked the woman, I wouldn't have wished that…"

Flora realised that Lizzie must have left before the most terrible events unfolded that day, "Yes, it has been quite a shock for everyone."

"I can imagine, please take a seat the food won't be long," Lizzie moved to a large Aga range, where two pots sat on the top rings, their contents bubbling away, "I've prepared us a beef stew with dumplings, I hope that'll be okay. I thought to make us something warming."

"That sounds perfect Lizzie, thank you so much," Flora took a moment to enjoy the huge room – the large, open plan kitchen, dining area and sitting room was painted white to emphasise the colourful artwork which was covering every wall. A skylight over the cooking area would bathe the space in extra light during the day, Flora imagined, admiring the sight of the dark sky above her through the glass.

"You didn't bring your friend with you?" Lizzie asked as she stirred.

Immediately thinking of Adam, Flora blushed before realising Lizzie must have meant Reggie, "Ah no, he's a bit out of sorts so I've left him to have some quiet time."

"Ah, bless him. Wine?" Lizzie asked.

"Best not, I'm driving," Flora said, somewhat regretfully.

"Of course, I've a homemade elderflower cordial? It's non-alcoholic."

"Perfect, these are beautiful pictures you have, are they all yours?"

"On this side of the room, yes, mostly," Lizzie left the stove to come and show Flora around. The walls matched Lizzie's own sense of style in that each painting was a riot of colours, yet they all seemed to come together to produce an overall effect which was classy and well thought out.

"I can see your work here in the animal paintings,"

Flora said, going straight to a series of portraits, very similar to that of Reggie, but featuring a myriad of creatures from dogs to a chameleon.

"Yes, they're mine, as are some of the landscapes, and these pieces are earlier, from my college days and just after."

Flora was intrigued by the development in style and form between Lizzie's first pieces and her later artworks. A couple of the framed pictures in this area seemed to stand out, in that they were highly skilled, more like animations really, but they didn't quite fit with the rest. Flora didn't want to appear so rude as to mention them, but Lizzie saw the direction of her gaze.

"Yes, those aren't mine, they're Martin's actually."

"Martin Loughbrough's?"

"Yes, he gifted them to me for my twenty-first birthday," Lizzie blushed and Flora got the hint of something in her tone, though she wasn't quite sure what.

"You were close?" Flora asked, trying not to appear nosy.

"We were friends, yes, but he only had eyes for Clarissa, even then, though she has never had the talent to match the size of her mouth. The latter was always much bigger!" Lizzie walked back to the kitchen area effectively killing the topic of conversation. This left Flora to ponder what her hostess had said as she admired the works on the other walls, which were by other local artists and some well-known painters. Flora had known that Lizzie and Clarissa had not seen eye to eye at university, or since, but hadn't considered until now that meant she would also have known Martin – and not just a passing acquaintance by the looks of it!

The two women chatted comfortably over the meal, of Lizzie's partner who worked in Edinburgh during the week and only came home for weekends, and of holiday plans. Flora felt a dull ache of remorse when she told Lizzie that she and Adam were hoping to have a break away together in the spring, though she didn't give any outward indication of this. Whilst she was friendly with Lizzie, Flora didn't feel close enough to her to spill all the details of her relationship woes. Instead, after Lizzie had produced a fantastic lemon meringue pie and served them both a healthy slice with cream – the diet would start another day, Flora decided, as it would be rude to refuse – their conversation turned to the coming week.

"Well, sadly I have the funeral of another artist friend

of mine, Gerald Castleford, who had a fatal fall last week."

"Yes, I may have read about that," Flora said, keeping her comment ambiguous as she didn't want to let on that Adam was the one investigating the case, which seemed to be more sinister than a simple fall would suggest.

"Poor man, about my age he was too, and so talented. He always had a kind word to say about everyone else's work too, he'll be a miss at the local art shows for sure," Lizzie looked sad.

"I'm so sorry," Flora added, "it reminds us of our own mortality when these things happen."

"It really does," a silence descended over them then, as both women pondered their own thoughts while they ate.

Not wanting to drive back too late, Flora found herself arriving back at the coach house at just before half past nine. As she turned into the driveway, which only this morning had hosted the press teams – *was that just this morning?* – Flora secretly hoped to see Adam's car waiting for her. In fact, if she was honest with herself, it was a main part of why she had come home earlier than planned. It was not to be, however, and she drove her own car into the empty spot closest to her door.

It was so lovely to come home to someone waiting for her, Flora thought, as the familiar beat of green wings came fast down the hallway having been heralded by the sound of her key in the old wooden door.

"My Flora!" Reggie cooed as he landed on Flora's head before she could even put her handbag down and begin taking off her coat.

"My Reggie," she replied, kicking off her smart shoes and walking straight to the kitchen with her feathered friend on her shoulder, "time for some wine, I think!"

"Wine time! Wine time!" Reggie chimed, like one of the antique clocks up at the manor house.

"It certainly is and I, for one, am ready for it!" Flora sat down in her favourite armchair, not even bothering to light the log burner. The central heating would warm the place up enough to be comfortable till she had her bath and from there went straight to bed.

For the first time that day, Flora actually had the time and space to relax, to stop and reflect, and suddenly memories of all the day's conversations came flooding back to her causing a lump to form in Flora's throat. The interview had been bad enough, and then that uncomfortable encounter with Gareth, but topping the lot by an easy mile was her conversation – her argument – with Adam. It was this that caused the tears to fall anew, worrying Flora's little friend again.

"My Flora! My Flora! Sad! Bad sad! Sad bad!" Reggie tried desperately to covey his sympathy and Flora was so touched by it that she picked him up in her hand, brought him close to her wet face and kissed his little head.

"Thank you, Reggie," she whispered, "I'm fine, really, and I've got no one but myself to blame. I need to learn to stop meddling and focus on my own life. Goodness knows, I've got enough to juggle."

Reggie cocked his head as he listened intently, and nuzzled his feathers against Flora's palm.

"What to do, Reggie, that is the question. Should I call Adam? Or wait for him to call me? I don't want to bother him while he's working the murder case over in Alnwick. What to do, What to do..."

"What to do," Reggie repeated, hopping from one foot to the other, as if he knew he had repeated the words correctly and was proud of himself.

Standing slowly, letting the parrot climb up her arm as she walked, Flora went into the kitchen and chopped a banana into pieces for him.

"Good bird," she said as she left Reggie munching through his treat on the kitchen table and turned off the lights in the hallway and sitting room. She wouldn't contact Adam today, Flora decided, not when they were both tired and frazzled, but maybe tomorrow.

There was always tomorrow.

TWENTY

Morning arrived with a thick frost and Flora had to force herself to get out of bed. Her head and her heart both felt weary, and she wasn't sure she could plaster her usual smile on her face and pretend to everyone that her world wasn't feeling bleak right now. Nevertheless, she ran the shower as hot as she could take it and stood there for a good fifteen minutes, hoping to revive her senses a bit, before having a breakfast of porridge and coffee. Jean from the shop was a staunch supporter of porridge for breakfast to set you up for the day – a legacy of her Scottish heritage, Flora surmised – and Flora had been persuaded to buy some oats the last time she popped in. She had to admit now that the warm meal felt hearty and Flora was in a slightly more positive frame of mind as she and Reggie set off for the tearoom, with him snuggled in his little portable carrier as protection from the freezing conditions.

Any good mood evaporated swiftly, however, when Flora found Phil waiting outside the shop for her.

"Ah, Flora, excellent timing, I just arrived but I have to be quick as I'm on the way to school."

"Okay," Flora hid her sigh inside her scarf, which was pulled up almost to her nose. She unlocked the door for them both and then hurried to turn on the heating. The little place was almost as cold inside as it was outside.

"It's the thick stone walls of the original stables that do it," Phil commented, shoving his gloved hands into his pockets.

"Do what?"

"Make it seem so cold," Phil was watching his own breath float away as he spoke.

"Well it'll warm up soon enough," Flora muttered, "what can I do for you, Phil?"

"Actually, I'm after some advice, and I couldn't think of anyone else..."

"If it's about adult literature, I'm really not in the

mood!"

"What? No! No, I realise that's something I need to pursue myself. You made that very clear. No, actually Flora it's to do with the investigation."

"The murder? I'm really not getting involved in that," *better late than never,* Flora thought as she indicated that they should both sit down, and she released Reggie to jump onto his perch. Except he didn't go to his perch, instead he landed directly on Phil's head and screeched "The fool has arrived!"

"Perch or back in your bag!" Flora said sternly, in no mood for his outbursts this morning, "Sorry Phil, I really don't think I can help."

"Well, ah, it's just that when the police interviewed me I held back a bit of information," the man pressed on as if Flora had simply not spoken at all.

"Really, why?" *And why is he telling me this, and not the police?* Flora wondered, feeling exasperated and wanting to simply end the conversation as quickly as possible.

"Well, do you remember when your ex-husband went missing and I had witnessed the two of you arguing. I felt so awful having to tell the police about that. I don't want to drop another neighbour in it so to speak."

"Which neighbour?" Flora didn't have the patience to skirt around the issue any longer. If Phil was determined to bare his soul, he needed to do it quickly.

"Gareth. I know he doesn't live in the village, but he is Amy's boyfriend and I..."

"What thing about Gareth did you hold back?" Flora asked, the sinking feeling returning to the pit of her stomach.

"Well, that day, the book event day, you will have seen me going out to talk to Ms. Cutter. She, ah, well she gave me short shrift and just as I was walking away, I thought to have another go at talking to her, but I turned round to see Gareth following her onto the path to the coach house so I gave up and came back inside."

"Oh," Flora's mind whirred as the implications of this sank in. Not least that Gareth had lied to Amy and to the police. And to herself yesterday.

"I just didn't want to drop anyone else in it," Phil continued, "but now I'm not so sure I've done the right thing. You're good with these police investigations, Flora, what do you think I should do?

"Well, I wouldn't exactly say I'm good with them, Phil.

I've dealt with them out of necessity rather than choice, but if you're asking my advice… I'd say be honest and tell the police what you know. Otherwise it may well come to bite you in the backside later," Flora's stomach sank further even as she said it, though she knew it was the right thing to do.

"Right then, right then," Phil squashed his knitted hat back over his unruly hair and stood up, "got to be getting to work. Thanks Flora."

He left to cries of "Good riddance!" from Reggie and Flora sat still for a moment, having neither the energy nor the enthusiasm to get up and face the day. Face it she must, though, so after a few minutes she began her morning tasks, trying to keep her mind on anything but the conversation she'd just had.

The rest of the morning passed quietly, and Flora even managed to take a small lunchbreak while Tanya manned the fort in the tearoom. Sitting with a cheese sandwich and a coffee in the empty bookshop, Flora scanned the few shelves of children's books, wondering morosely if she would ever see her own work there amongst them one day. She hadn't even picked up the manuscripts of her children's stories since Clarissa's murder, and the vintage typewriter which had been on show for the opening event was now safely ensconced back in its box at the coach house, with Flora feeling unable to get it out again. Her muse, her inspiration, whatever one wanted to call it, had shrivelled up and gone into hiding. Something Flora dearly hoped would only be a temporary setback.

A large picture book caught Flora's eye, as it had Clarissa's name as the illustrator in bold gold script on the spine along with the author. Flora picked it out on a whim and flicked through it. She had no idea why, other than to make herself feel even worse. The pictures seemed familiar, and Flora thought she must have read the book before maybe to the Marshall girls, though she had no recollection of the story. No, it was the illustrations themselves which jolted her memory, and Flora jumped up suddenly rushing to the desk drawer and taking out the pencil drawings she had stored there from the other day.

Holding a picture of a mother dragon with her egg up against the same illustration in the book, Flora was shocked to see that they were almost identical. There could be no doubt that the same artist had made both. And that artist, Flora knew for certain, was Martin Loughbrough and not Clarissa Cutter, for it had been he who had been drawing in the bookshop with the girls on Monday.

Confused by this new knowledge, but knowing it must be true as she could see the evidence with her own eyes, Flora wondered what she should do now. Ordinarily, she would phone Adam and ask for his advice but Flora felt she couldn't do that – with their relationship in unchartered territory and his radio silence, Flora didn't want to bother him with this. She could just imagine how the uncomfortable conversation would go. Instead, she took the sensible path for once, and phoned Detective McArthur. Flora still had the detective's card in her purse under the counter in the tearoom and so she took that and her mobile phone back into the bookshop with her where she could get some privacy. The vicar was in the tearoom, deep in conversation with a parishioner, so Flora simply waved as she rushed through.

"And you are sure?" McArthur asked when Flora had explained her findings.

"As sure as I can be. You are very welcome to take the book and the drawings."

"Yes, we'll definitely have to do that. Blackett and I are busy interviewing at the moment, so I'll send an officer across to get them and to take a quick statement."

"Very well, I'll look out for them."

"Oh, and Ms. Miller…"

"Yes?"

"Thank you for bringing this straight to our attention."

"You're welcome," though Flora felt a bit sick as she ended the call. She wondered if the interview the detective had mentioned was with Gareth, though perhaps Phil had not called them with his own information yet. Perhaps he would wait till the end of the school day.

Flora didn't know. In truth, she wasn't sure she wanted to know. She felt drained with investigations and evidence and the whole lot of it. She certainly couldn't even contemplate phoning Amy with what she had learnt from Gareth and subsequently Phil. Once the officer had come and got what they needed, Flora decided she would close up both shops and go home, put her feet up for a couple of hours until she went to Lily's for dinner at the farm.

Yes, hiding away seemed like the best option right now and Flora was determined not to feel guilty about it.

TWENTY-ONE

Flora opted to drive to the farm that evening, feeling too weary to walk even after a couple of hours' rest, though she went at about ten miles an hour to account for the extremely icy roads. As she pulled up outside the farmhouse after bumping and bouncing her way along the farm track, Flora saw Stan coming out of the cow shed with his faithful sheepdog, Bertie, at his heel.

"Evenin' Flora, Lily's expectin' yer," Stan was a man of few words, and Flora thought she could count on one hand the number of times she'd heard him speak since coming to the village.

"Thank you, Stan," Flora took off her boots as the farmhouse door opened and Lily enveloped her in a warm hug.

"There you are Flora, I was worried about you getting here with the ice an' all."

"Well, it was a bit tricky once I was out of the village, The Rear End felt like a single sheet of ice, but I'm here now!" To be honest, the drive had been awful, and Flora had regretted it as soon as she'd got onto the lane from the coach house driveway, but she didn't want her friend to feel bad.

"Aye well, you'll need to be careful going back. The conditions will be even worse by then as the temperature drops," Stan said, coming into the house behind the women, "I can tek you back in the tractor if you like."

"No, no I'm sure I'll be fine," Flora said, though already she was beginning to worry about the journey back.

Lily served up a deep chicken and leek pie with mashed potatoes, peas and gravy, followed by a homemade jam roly-poly and custard, which meant the conversation was scarce as they all tucked in to the hearty fare.

"My goodness, Lily, I'm stuffed!" Flora declared, "That

was beautiful, thank you!"

"Aye, she's the best cook my Lily," Stan said, excusing himself from the table and settling into his well-worn chair by the open fire, Bertie going to lie at his feet.

Flora wondered if Stan ever did any of the housework or cooking, but then he was working all day on the farm and Lily seemed happy enough in her role here and running the farm shop. *Who am I to comment on what most would consider their old-fashioned set up?* Flora asked herself, *my own relationship is hardly a shining example of what to do and how to do it!*

"A penny for them," Lily said gently, remaining in her seat and giving Flora an inquisitive look.

"Oh, well, it's a lot of things… the investigation and all, but mainly," Flora looked around to see if Stan was listening, but he was busy watching an old episode of 'Countryfile,' "mainly Adam."

"Oh?" Lily asked gently.

"Yes, we had a falling out."

"Over that interview?"

"You saw that?"

"I think all of Northumberland saw it," Lily gave a wry

smile and rubbed Flora's arm, "but it's done now and it's not worth you and Adam falling out over."

"Well, it wasn't just that," Flora sighed, "I did something I said I wouldn't do, and in doing so broke a promise I'd made him. It's our first real fight and he hasn't spoken to me since."

"I see, well, only the two of you can know if it was a deal breaker or not, but my advice would be to at least talk to him about it. The longer it goes on the bigger the distance between you will seem, and what perhaps started as a molehill can quickly become a mountain."

Flora knew that Lily was right. At the very least, she and Adam needed to say their amicable goodbyes. So why did the thought of losing him make her feel sick to her stomach?

"My ex, Gregory, and I had many arguments, of course, but I think the difference was that neither of us really cared whether we got past them or not. We lived quite separate lives so it was barely even noticeable when we weren't on talking terms with each other."

"Aye, Stan and I have had some corkers over the years, but we both felt bad until we'd made up again. I guess that's the question, do you like him enough to work though it?"

"I love him," Flora whispered, "I want nothing more than for it all go back to how it was between us."

"Well, things might not go back, maybe they'll be stronger and better going forward if you can air your grievances and work through them."

"You're a wise woman, Lily," Flora gave a small laugh.

"Aye well, you're not the first to say so!" Lily joked, blushing.

The women cleared the table and washed the dishes before sharing a pot of tea, and Stan went out to check on the animals one last time for the day, making sure before he went that Flora didn't want any help getting home.

"No, no, I'll be fine, thanks," Flora replied, though perhaps she should have listened to the butterflies in her stomach which were jittery about the upcoming journey.

Even the fact that she had to de-ice her car before she could even think about driving it home, did nothing to change Flora's mind about setting off alone. Once she was past the farm track and onto the main route to Baker's rise, Flora realised suddenly what the difference between driving on icy roads in the city at this time of year was, compared to doing exactly the same thing out here in the countryside – the lights. Or rather, the lack of them. These country lanes were pitch black on a night in this area, which made them seem even more foreboding despite Flora inching along at what seemed a snail's pace.

Flora's hands gripped the wheel tighter as she came along the bit of road in Baker's Bottom where Gregory's car had veered into the trees on the other side at the end of last year. As she was distracted for a moment looking across to the other empty lane and beyond it to the sparse woods, a deer darted out from the bushes on her own side of the road, and Flora quickly swerved to avoid it. In doing so, the car skidded on the icy road and ended up in the deep ditch which ran alongside. Thankfully, Flora was going so slowly that what could have been a major accident was instead just a quick inflation of her airbag from the impact of the front of the car hitting the bottom of the ditch. A quick glance through her fogged side window told Flora the deer was fine and long gone, for which she was grateful. That didn't help her own predicament, though, and Flora tried to calm the frantic beating of her panicked heart as she scrabbled in the footwell of the passenger side for her handbag.

After several long moments, Flora located her phone in her bag and saw that she had three missed calls from Adam. She had forgotten that she had put her phone on silent, out of politeness, when she had arrived at the farmhouse. That couldn't be helped now, though, as Flora had no intention of calling Adam and asking him to be her knight in shining armour. Besides, she had friends more locally who could help. That is, if she could find a signal. This area of Northumberland was notoriously bad for mobile phone coverage, and despite waving her phone above her head at odd angles, Flora couldn't find even a weak enough signal to make a call.

Forcing an optimism she really didn't feel, Flora fastened her winter coat and, ignoring everything she had ever been told about being in an accident – namely to stay in the car – she ventured tentatively out of the vehicle. The car being at the odd angle that it was, Flora had first to squeeze through the tiny gap that was all the door would open against the side of the ditch, and then use her hands to hoist herself up the ditch itself, grappling against the frozen grass with her feet. Despite sliding back down a couple of times, Flora persisted, until she found herself on her hands and knees on the road itself. Holding the phone above her head, Flora had a few choice words to say when still no signal bar showed up. Deciding resolutely that she was committed to this course of action now, however, Flora slowly managed to get to her feet. *Surely there'll be a signal somewhere along here?*

When skidding a few feet along the road brought her no luck, Flora had what she would later refer to as her 'insane idea' – to go back into the ditch, climb up the other side and see if the ground was any higher there, nearer the trees. On trying to slide back down into the ditch, just behind her car, however, Flora's left foot caught a particularly icy patch of grass and slipped out faster than she could stop it. As her foot hit the bottom of the ditch it collapsed sideways and Flora heard the crunch in the still night air as her ankle took the brunt of the pressure.

"Ahh!" Flora shouted, her breath misting in front of her as she lay on the freezing floor of the ditch, unable to get up. Her head whirred with a dozen different things – the pain, of course, but also her own stupidity at getting out of the car, how she was likely to be murdered or to freeze to death on this deserted road as she surely wouldn't be found before morning…

Just as she thought it, Flora saw some headlights coming up the road towards her. Dim and distant at first, they were soon close enough to blind her. Half of

Flora prayed that they would spot her car and come looking. Then she could shout for help. The other half of her – the one fixated on the whole murder scenario – prayed that they would simply drive past.

Flora had no choice but to wait and see which prayer would be answered.

TWENTY-TWO

With the cold and the pain and the shock, Flora found herself drifting in and out of consciousness. At times she thought she heard Adam's voice, which must surely be her head playing tricks on her, yet nevertheless it gave Flora comfort. She heard the sirens as if from a foggy dream and only barely felt it when she was lifted up and out of the ditch and had something sharp put into her arm. The rest was a blur, of being in something which moved quickly, of a reassuring pressure on her hand, and Adam's voice – always Adam's voice – steady and constant.

"Flora, love, are you awake?"

Flora forced her eyes to open, blinking against the

bright overhead lights, "Adam?"

"I'm here love, I'm here. You're at the hospital, they're coming to wheel you down to get your ankle x-rayed. My God, Flora, you gave me the fright of my life. First seeing your car in that state and then you being nowhere to be found at first…"

"How did you?"

"Oh, I used the torch on my phone and…"

"No, how did you find me on that road? Why were you coming along there at nine o'clock at night?"

"Because I'd been trying to call you all evening, and when I got no reply I decided to come and say it face to face. I thought you couldn't ignore me so easily if I was there on your doorstep."

"I wasn't ignoring you. I was at the farm, had my phone on silent," Flora's throat felt dry and her voice croaked.

Adam reached over to gently wipe her face with his thumbs and Flora realised that she was crying.

"Aw sweetheart, thank goodness it was me who found you, it doesn't bear thinking about if..," he squeezed Flora's hand, and as her eyes acclimatised to her surroundings, Flora saw that Adam's eyes too looked a bit watery, "If anything had happened to you…"

"Shh, I'm fine, and I'm right here. When I didn't hear from you yesterday or earlier today I thought maybe that was it for us."

"What? No, I was phoning you tonight to say I missed you, and I love you and I didn't want us to fall out. We can talk about it, when you're better, and move on."

"Really?"

"Of course… if it's what you want?" he seemed a little unsure of himself now, and it would have been endearing if Flora didn't feel so guilty for everything – the argument, her actions which had caused it, this accident.

"Of course it's what I want, I don't deserve you."

"Thank goodness. And I don't want to hear you say that nonsense again!" Adam kissed her lips softly and Flora tasted her own tears between them. The sweet moment was broken by the porter coming to take Flora to x-ray, though at her request Adam accompanied her to the waiting room.

"Reggie!" Flora blurted when she was back in Accident & Emergency in her little cubicle.

"Don't worry, love, I called Pat Hughes and he's going to get Harry's spare key first thing in the morning and then bring Reggie down to their house for him and Tanya to look after. She'll take him to the tearoom with her."

"But he'll be by himself all night!"

"There's not much of the night left now, love and you know you're going to have to stay in at least until the consultant can look at your x-rays and see if you're going to need surgery on that ankle. Reggie will be asleep by now, probably none the wiser, and you always leave seed and water attached to his cage, don't you?"

"Yes, but… aw my poor bird, he'll sulk for a week over this."

"Well, the main thing is that we get you sorted, isn't it? So that you can get back to him."

The pain relief that the paramedics had given her was wearing off and Flora's tolerance seemed to be declining as her bad temper was building. Worried that she might snap at Adam, who had been nothing but lovely to her, not even remonstrating with her about the stupidity of her actions, Flora laid her head back and closed her eyes. The hellish throb in her ankle and up her leg was nothing less than she deserved, Flora decided, and she lay there feeling very sorry for herself.

It was three o'clock the next afternoon when Adam opened the door to the coach house, before coming back to help Flora out of his car. With the aid of crutches, and Adam's steadying hand on her back so that he could grab her if she slipped, Flora hopped slowly into the house. Thankfully, she hadn't needed surgery, but her ankle was certainly broken and she had been given a delightful moon boot to wear.

"I'll get you settled and then I'll go and get our little feathered friend from the tearoom," Adam said, helping Flora into the armchair, "other than that, though, I'm not letting you out of my sight until we go to the fractures clinic at the Northumbria Hospital in Cramlington tomorrow."

"But what about your case?"

"I'm off duty today and tomorrow anyway, and I'll phone to let them know I won't be in on Saturday, we've followed up all the leads we have so far, so they'll just be consolidating the evidence."

"No, Adam, I'll be fine by the weekend. If you're concerned you could ask some of the neighbours to pop in."

"We'll see. For now, please just let me help you."

"Okay, thank you. And Adam?"

"Yes?"

" I love you, I'm so sorry."

"Please stop apologising, I love you and I want to make sure you're okay. When I think of what could have happened..!"

"Shh I know, I was stupid, it's the quiet life for me from now on, I promise."

"I'm very glad to hear that," Adam bent to kiss her forehead after arranging the throw blanket over Flora's knees and lifting her booted foot onto a stool, "now, let me get our little Reggie from Tanya, no doubt he's given her a memorable day!"

"Oh goodness, yes!"

With Reggie back home where he should be, and having tried to reassure him with snuggles and a monumental fruit salad prepared by Adam, Flora found herself dozing off on the chair.

"I'm sorry," she mumbled, "can't seem to keep my eyes open."

"Don't be silly, your body needs rest to heal, I'll be here," Adam said softly.

"My Flora!" Reggie squawked from his perch. Not nearly so sulky as Flora had worried he might be, he seemed more worried than anything.

"Good bird," Flora whispered as she nodded off.

Perhaps it was the pain medication she had been given, but Flora's dreams were vivid and fast paced, jumping from the bookshop to Clarissa to Martin to Lizzie and then to Gareth and Amy. Thoroughly shaken, she woke up with a fine sheen of sweat over her brow and the blanket knotted around her arms.

"Hey what's this?" Adam asked, coming in from the kitchen and followed by a glorious smell of something cooking.

Flora's heart beat quickly in her chest making her feel sick. She lifted her hand to her mouth and Adam rushed back into the kitchen to grab a bowl for her. As Adam stroked her hair back, and Flora took several deep breaths, she began to feel slightly better, letting her head sink onto his shoulder where he knelt beside her.

"Sorry, bad dreams," Flora croaked.

"About the accident?"

"No, funnily enough, they weren't about last night. It was like a movie reel of everything from before Clarissa's death until now."

"Oh love, try not to think about it."

"I will, it's just… how do you manage it? Not bringing the awful cases you deal with home with you?"

"It's hard, and I admit I do re-visit some of them in my dreams," Adam said sadly, "but that's my job, I chose it, you need to focus on the things that make you happy – your writing, your little bird and your shops."

"And you, you come top of that list," Flora said, "but there have been a couple of developments in the murder case, can I tell you about them? I came upon them without any investigating of my own, I promise."

"Go on then, but after that no more mentioning it!" Adam looked at Flora indulgently and she smiled back.

Flora told him about what Phil had said about Gareth

following Clarissa, and what she herself had discovered about Martin's illustrative skills.

"Well, those certainly add extra dimensions, and I'm sure Blackett and McArthur will be following them up, you did the right thing contacting them. Now that it's off your chest, do you think you can rest again while I go and finish that spaghetti bolognese I'm cooking for us?"

Flora nodded and made the clicking sound with her mouth that was the signal for Reggie to come and join her. He flew over immediately, his greens and yellows glinting in the low afternoon sun that came through the old windows.

"My Reggie," Flora said as he nuzzled into her neck, and her eyelids became heavy again.

TWENTY-THREE

Friday was a long, difficult day of hospital appointments and travelling, as the specialist hospital was nearly an hour away on the wintery roads. Adam drove slowly and tried to avoid any bumps that might jiggle Flora's leg, but even so she was sore and exhausted when they got back to the coach house.

"So, about tomorrow," Flora began when she was settled back in her chair with Reggie perched beside her, "I really will be fine while you go into work."

They had taken a rather long detour after the hospital to drop by Adam's apartment in Morpeth and pick up his work clothes and other toiletries.

"I just don't want to leave you yet," Adam said,

turning from where he was lighting the log burner, a frown on his face.

"I know, and you have been so brilliant, but really I'll be okay. I'm managing to walk about the house on my crutches."

"Well, let's compromise. You give me the numbers for Betty, Tanya, Sally and Amy and I'll see what I can organise."

So it was arranged that Betty and Harry would sit with Flora for the morning on Saturday, Tanya would open the tearoom from ten till two, Sally and the girls would look after the bookshop between those hours, and Amy would come across after lunch to give Flora's hair a trim and hopefully perk her up a bit.

Flora had to admit that she did feel better when it was all organised, knowing that she wouldn't be alone when Adam was at work. Currently, her worst fear was falling and not being able to get up.

"Keep your mobile phone in your pocket at all times too," Adam told her, "I'll have mine and you can call me any time, you understand?"

Flora nodded and squeezed his hand, tears of gratitude filling her eyes.

"Hey, no tears, it's all going to work out fine. Peace and quiet, rest and recuperation, and when you're feeling better I can help you decide what to do with the manor house. I know it's been weighing on your mind."

"It has, yes, thank you Adam. For everything."

Saturday dawned with the promise of being a beautiful winter's day, clear and crisp – the perfect day for staying cosied up at home and watching the winter sun through the window. It lifted Flora's spirits, though not as much as the note she found on the kitchen counter from Adam, who had risen before dawn to get into the station. Smiling as she read it, Flora made herself a cup of coffee and hobbled back to the sitting room. Putting her coffee on the table next to her favourite armchair, Flora hopped the few steps to the antique bookcase that had been in the property when she inherited it. She couldn't help but grin at the ridiculously garish teapot Tanya had given her for Christmas. It was in the shape of a parrot head, with the beak being the spout, the head feathers as the lid and the handle one long feather. It was even the same colours as Reggie! Tanya had said she'd found it in the charity shop in Witherham and couldn't resist. The thing was certainly not made from fine china, as it weighed a ton! It must be some kind of pottery, Flora thought absentmindedly as she chose her favourite, well-thumbed copy of 'Pride and Prejudice' and sat back down, hoisting her booted leg back onto her foot stool.

"Visitors! Visitors with money!" Reggie shrieked, causing Flora to jerk awake. Realising she must've dozed off again, as her book was open on her chest and her coffee long gone cold, Flora was met with the smiling faces of Betty and Harry.

"Aw Flora, what have you done to yerself now?" Betty asked, fussing like a mother hen, "Harry, get that kettle on, tea is what's needed here to perk her up, and plate up those scones I've brought! Look how pale the lass is!"

"I'm fine, Betty, really, the doctor said I'd feel tired while my bone heals."

"Aye well, we're here now to keep you company. You've got a good'un there in that Adam, making sure we would all rally around you. But I would have come, you know, even if he hadn't asked!"

"I know, Betty, I know," Flora smiled, letting the older woman tuck the blanket round her snugly.

When they were all settled around the fire with hot tea and scones with jam and cream, Betty embarked on her favourite subject – village gossip.

"So, did you hear that young Amy had another funny turn? At work in the hairdresser's it was, my friend Mrs. May was having her monthly perm and set, when Amy had to run and be sick in one of the sinks. She said it was the smell of the perming solution, and we all know what that means!" Betty gave another of those knowing looks, the ones she had shared with Tanya but which Flora had forgotten to ask about.

"Do we? I'm not sure I do," Flora said, perplexed.

"Well, increased sense of smell can be an early sign of… you know!"

"I really don't."

"That she's got a babby on the way! That and the fainting, it all makes sense!" Betty looked very pleased with herself, as Harry sighed from where he was secretly feeding the raisins from his fruit scone to Reggie.

"Oh! Do you think Amy knows?"

"Not from what Hilda May said, she told me the girl was confused as the smell of that solution has never had that effect on her before."

"Well, since it's just speculation, we should probably keep it to ourselves," Flora said, setting her cup down and yawning, "I'm so sorry Betty, I'm going to have to have a little nap."

"You go on, dear, we'll make ourselves busy with a bit of polishing and hoovering," Harry said kindly, as Flora's head drooped.

Flora was woken gently by Betty a couple of hours later, as Harry stood beside her with a tray of lunchtime sandwiches.

"I'm so sorry, how rude of me, I didn't mean to sleep so long, must be the painkillers," Flora said.

"That reminds me, Adam says you're to have some more tablets about now," Harry said, as he laid the tray on the coffee table and disappeared back into the kitchen.

"Oh, I don't really need to, they'll just make me sleepy again," Flora said.

"That's as may be, but you have to keep on top of the pain," Harry said gently, and Flora accepted the glass of water and box of painkillers.

They shared the sandwiches and chatted – which mainly consisted of Flora and Harry listening to Betty's complaints about Edwina Edwards and the woman's perceived failings as chairwoman of the local W.I.

"Well I think we've bore… ah, we've entertained Flora long enough," Harry said, as he came in from washing their lunch plates in the kitchen, "Amy will be here in a minute, so we'll be off, shall we?"

"Thank you both so much for coming," Flora said, as she let out another huge yawn. Her head felt fuzzy and she could tell the new dose of painkillers was starting to work.

"We'll leave the door unlocked for Amy, so she can just come in then you don't have to get up," Harry said thoughtfully, as Betty bustled about making sure the TV controls were within Flora's reach.

"Bye then," Flora whispered, which was the last thing she remembered until she and Reggie were both startled awake by a hammering on the front door.

"Come in," Flora shouted through the fog in her brain, expecting it to be Amy.

Imagine her surprise, therefore when it wasn't the friendly hairdresser, but instead a rather angry-looking

Martin Loughbrough who strode confidently into her little sitting room.

TWENTY-FOUR

"Somebody else!" Reggie squawked unhappily, and Flora shared his sentiments. Her gut told her this wasn't just a social visit, and as Martin sat on the settee opposite her, without removing either his coat or leather gloves, Flora had no choice but to sit and listen.

"Good afternoon, Flora," Martin said, polite as always.

"Hello, Martin, I'm rather indisposed at the moment, as you can see," Flora hoped to get rid of the man as quickly as possible, so planned to dispense with the pleasantries.

"Yes, I called into the tearoom to see you, and that strange Russian woman told me you were at home with a broken leg."

"It's my ankle and she's Ukrainian," Flora corrected, though she had no idea why she was bothering.

"Well, never mind, if it was a sickbed visit I'd have brought fruit and flowers. As it is, I was wanting to talk to you about some drawings."

"Drawings?" Flora feigned ignorance, though she knew exactly the illustrations which Martin was referring to.

"Yes, I've had some very interesting conversations with our friendly local detectives these past couple of days. They seem to think I am the one who has been doing the artwork all this time, and not our dear departed Clarissa. I wonder how they got those drawings I did in your bookshop, Flora?"

Flora remained silent, as they both knew how the pictures had come to be in the hands of the police. Her head was thumping and her eyes were heavy. She just needed him to leave.

"Don't play dumb, Flora, we both know you gave them the lead. What I want to know, is what other ideas are going round that little head of yours?"

"Excuse me?"

"What else have you been figuring out all by yourself

and have you shared it with anyone?"

"I have no idea what you're referring to!" Flora was starting to feel the beginning of panic deep down in her gut. She surreptitiously felt the pocket of her wide skirt, and was reassured to feel her mobile phone there. It would take the usual monumental effort for her to lift her leg down from the stool and to get out of the chair, so for the moment she was pretty much pinned here and forced to listen to Martin for as long as he wanted.

Martin smiled, but it was a cold expression which came nowhere near reaching his eyes, "Have you ever been in love, Flora?" he asked.

Flora's befuddled brain could barely keep up with the change in subject, but she replied, "Yes, once."

"To the delectable Detective Bramble, no doubt," his tone was scoffing, "well I too have only been in love once. With a young woman I met at art college."

"Clarissa," Flora whispered.

"The very same. I imagine you have no idea what it's like to live with your feelings unrequited for over thirty years," Flora remained silent, so he continued, "oh, I tried putting physical distance between us by living abroad for twenty of those years, but my feelings didn't diminish with time or distance."

"So, why did you come back and work with her of all things?" Flora asked, unable to help herself.

"Well, Clarissa and I met again by chance ten years ago – actually, since we're being honest here, that's a lie, I orchestrated the whole meeting at a local gallery, there was nothing chance about it – and we caught up over coffees and the like. Imagine my surprise when she confided in me that her sight was failing and she was going to have to start giving up her illustrative work in favour of doing more articles and reviews of others' art. Seeing my way in, I offered to do the drawings for her, if she took me on as her personal assistant. By being close to her every day in this capacity, I thought she'd eventually come to love me the way I did her. Especially since I was keeping her big secret for her so that she held onto her reputation as a talented illustrator."

"And did she? Love you back, I mean," Flora whispered.

"No," Martin's face hardened into someone that Flora didn't recognise, "no, she did not. Not even when that fool Castleford worked out our little secret and threatened to expose me as the real artist. I couldn't let him embarrass Clarissa like that, obviously, so I did what needed to be done."

"You killed Gerald Castleford?" Flora felt sick. It couldn't be a good sign that Martin was confiding in her like this. He surely couldn't let her live with this incriminating knowledge.

"I did, to please Clarissa, and you'd think she'd have been happy! But do you know what she said?"

Flora remained silent.

Martin carried on regardless – he was in full flow now, "She said that I was starting to scare her! Me, who had done nothing but adore her for my whole adult life!"

"What happened that day after the event, Martin?" Flora tried not to let her voice wobble, "What happened to Clarissa?"

"I waited till that fool teacher had gone, and that angry, burly bloke, who followed her for a moment then seemed to think better of it and went back in the other direction, then I caught up to Clarissa and of course sympathised with how you had all treated her. I was always pouring oil on troubled waters you see. Well, the bitch told me she needed space, that she was sick of me constantly suffocating her and acting like a lovesick puppy. That she no longer recognised the man I'd become, simpering one minute and raging the next."

"That was harsh," Flora said, trying to appease the man, who was now pacing wildly, though she knew it was in vain.

Reggie had started flying loops of the room, divebombing Martin's head, and Flora worried for her little friend's safety as much as her own.

"Harsh isn't the word. She broke my heart in that spilt second. Anyway, I had the tailors' shears in my pocket – I'd heard you all talking about them earlier in the bookshop and knew where your stupid detective put them – I'd taken them secretly after that bloke's outburst, when I'd heard him shouting at my Clarissa about how she upset his dead wife or some such nonsense. Anyway, when I saw him deciding not to follow her, and instead heading up towards that big house on the hill, I planned to follow him and make him pay, once I'd checked Clarissa was alright."

"But you used them on her instead?"

"Well, in the moment, I… and what of it?" He was shouting now, "Hadn't I suffered enough from her?"

Flora sat silently, willing her trembling body to calm. She needed to try to think her way out of this.

"Anyway," Martin took a deep breath and snarled at Reggie who was flying directly at his face now, "You stupid bird!"

He swatted at the parrot, but Reggie swooped out of the way in time, to Flora's relief. As Martin untied the silk cravat from around his neck and advanced on Flora, a menacing look in his eyes, the front door swung open and Amy shouted, "Just me!"

Martin, seeing his moment of opportunity disappearing, lunged at Flora. The whisky fumes from her attacker's breath were quite overpowering, as Reggie landed on the man's head, effectively blinding him with his open wings.

"Quick Amy, help, in here!" Flora shouted.

As her friend came into the room, and Martin shoved aside the bird pecking at his scalp, Flora watched helplessly as Martin caught Amy off guard and pushed her roughly into the wooden bookcase. Her eyes wide in shock, Amy banged her head on a shelf and sank down slowly, her knees buckling underneath her body.

"No! Amy!" Flora screamed, as Martin turned to face

her once again. As all his attention was focused on fighting Flora, who was desperately trying to stop the man from securing the tie about her neck, a loud crash sent their attacker sprawling to the floor.

Turning to the side, Flora saw Amy standing, holding onto the bookshelf for support and with the remains of the cracked parrot teapot – which had, by the looks of it, just made heavy contact with Martin's head – in her hands.

"Thank goodness, thank you, Amy, thank you, are you okay?" Flora asked, as Amy sank to her knees once again, "I'll phone Pat Hughes and get him to bring Dr. Edwards," Flora said, praying Amy was okay.

That had been a close call, much closer than Flora would like to admit, and she found herself sobbing through her phone calls, the second of which was to Adam. Help was on its way, and Amy was still conscious, resting her head on the side of Flora's chair. As long as Martin remained out for the count, they would be okay.

"Reggie, Reggie my boy," Flora whispered to the little bird who was sitting on the carpet looking somewhat stunned. With a full-body ruffle of his feathers and a shake of his little head, Reggie flew across and landed on Flora's arm.

"My Flora," he chirped softly, and the three of them waited in silence for help to arrive.

TWENTY-FIVE

Pat Hughes arrived first on the scene with Frank, who did several circuits of the small house, sniffing in every corner whilst Flora gave the police officer the most concise description she could manage. As Martin came round, he found himself already in handcuffs, with Dr. Edwards and Adam arriving shortly after.

"I thought you were having a quiet day, rest and recuperation remember?" Adam said to lighten the tone as he took in the sight of Flora. The worry lines across his brow were as prominent as she had ever seen them, however, and Flora knew he was trying to mask his own concern with his false joviality. Pat and the doctor helped Amy to Flora's bedroom, so that her banged head could be examined, as Flora explained to

Adam what Martin had revealed.

"So he definitely admitted to my Alnwick murder as well?" Adam asked, his tone incredulous.

"Yes, definitely, my medication may be strong, but I wouldn't imagine something like that!" Flora replied, indignant. In truth, though, she was not annoyed, simply extremely relieved and grateful to be alive. Martin had been taken into custody by officers who had arrived shortly after the others, with sirens blazing. No doubt the whole village would know that something was happening up here on The Rise and tongues would've already started wagging.

As if summoned by that thought, Tanya arrived just as Flora was finishing her explanation.

"Flora! What has happened? I have just closed the tearoom and seen the police cars racing through the village!"

"Well, I managed to catch another murderer," Flora admitted, rather sheepishly, "though it honestly wasn't my intention, I was just sitting here."

"You are like a magnet for them!" Tanya laughed at her own joke, just as her husband emerged from the bedroom.

"The doc's giving her the once over," Pat said, putting his arm around Tanya's waist and giving her a brief kiss on the forehead before spotting Adam and becoming all professional again.

"Who?" Tanya asked.

"Oh, unfortunately Amy got caught up in it too," Flora felt awful about that, though if it hadn't been for the younger woman, she herself probably wouldn't be here to tell the tale.

As if the room wasn't crowded enough, Blackett and McArthur arrived on the scene then, bringing with them an even darker cloud to cast over the whole affair.

"I'm not sure Flora's up to giving her statement just yet," Adam spoke up before Blackett could say anything, though the thunderous look on his face spoke for itself.

"Well, just a few questions…" McArthur began.

"Later," Adam said firmly, as Flora yawned and her pounding headache made her squint to get everyone into focus.

Taking the hint, Pat and Tanya offered to help Amy get home as the doctor had said she was fine for now, but he would recommend she pop into the surgery on Monday for some blood tests.

"Thank you so much, Amy," Flora grasped the young woman's trembling hand as she came to say goodbye, "I owe you a huge afternoon tea at the tearoom – you and Gareth."

The two detectives weren't so keen to leave, and it took Adam bluntly asking them to go before they would make a move. Even then, it was only with Flora's promise of an interview the next morning that they agreed to leave her in peace for now. As she was currently indisposed by way of her leg, they agreed to take the statement at the coach house, and also for Adam to be present, so Flora finally sat back, relieved that for today at least her duties were over.

It was four days later and Flora was making her first trip out of the house and down to the tearoom, with Adam's help of course. She was excited to be semi-mobile again, though the big boot remained and would do so for another month at least. Breathing in deeply of the late-afternoon, fresh country air, and enjoying the sight of Reggie soaring above them, Flora squeezed Adam's arm where they were linked at the elbow.

"Thank you for making this possible," she said happily.

"Not at all, it'll do you good to get out and see your friends. You've certainly had to put up with enough police visits over the last few days. At least that's all over now, and they got Loughbrough's confession yesterday."

"Yes, I can't tell you what a relief it is to know he's securely behind bars," Flora shuddered at the memory of the man's face as he tried to wrap the cravat around her neck, to add strangulation to his list of offences. Thanks to Amy's bravery he hadn't been successful, and that was the reason for the special visit to the tearoom today.

Betty and Lily had helped Tanya with the café over the past few days when they could, and they had all worked together to bake a beautiful afternoon tea for today. Flora entered the tearoom to find three of her small tables pushed together and covered in a fresh linen tablecloth, beautifully hand-embroidered, and which Jean said she had been keeping in a drawer for a special occasion. Everyone was there waiting for her – Amy and Gareth with Lewis, Tanya and Pat, Jean, Betty and Harry, Lily and Stan, Shona, Will and Aaron, and of course Sally with the girls.

"Please help yourselves everyone," Flora said, smiling around at her friends, "this afternoon tea is a thank you to you all for your help and support since I arrived in the village. For your friendship and for welcoming me into the community. In particular, though, it's to say thank you to Amy for her bravery the other day."

Amy blushed as everyone clapped for her, and Gareth kissed her soundly on the cheek, looking happier and more relaxed than Flora had ever seen him.

"We're so glad to see you looking so well," Sally said, as Flora took the seat next to her and they all began to tuck into the scones, cakes and sandwiches which were placed up and down the table on pretty china cake stands. Adam walked around, pouring cups of tea and Reggie made the most of the attention, waddling up and down the table and squawking, "Welcome to the tearoom" as if he owned the place!

"I'm just relieved to be here," Flora admitted, and she blinked back the few tears which threatened to escape. Her emotions were still raw whenever anyone gave her sympathy or reminded her of the past week's ordeal, "do you have any news?"

"Well, I plucked up the courage and organised a coffee morning for all the ladies of the local W.I. on Monday morning just gone at the church hall," Sally whispered, and Flora could tell she was angling her head so that Betty wouldn't overhear, "I decided to nip this leadership problem in the bud, as it just wasn't good for the community, especially the older residents who rely on the ladies for visits and lunches."

"You're brave," Flora raised her eyebrows, "how did it go?"

"Better than I thought actually. I had an idea that Betty and some of her friends were going to stage a coup to topple Edwina, so to speak, as chairwoman, so I decided to pre-empt them and suggest a whole restructuring of the local group," Sally's hushed whisper had Flora wanting to giggle. It was like they were talking secret tactics in a war room.

"And did they accept your idea?" Flora wanted to know.

"Well, not immediately, but I think I've won them over. They're going to vote on it at the meeting next week. I suggested that instead of one woman in charge, that we have a committee with different people responsible for different things – Jean for crafts, Edwina for parish communications, Betty for senior socials and so on."

"Wow, that's a great idea."

"I hoped you'd think so, Flora, as I was wondering if you'd agree to join and be our parish events organiser? Tanya has said she would do the talent show again, and so if you could organise the summer fete, some jumble sales and the like..?" Sally looked hopeful.

"It would be my pleasure," Flora said, "and what's your role, other than vicar's wife and mum of three, of course?"

"Well, at the moment it's peacekeeper!" Sally joked and both women laughed. Flora felt good to be laughing in her little tearoom again. It was so lovely to feel it buzzing with life and chatter and to watch the children as they ran between the tearoom and shop, with Reggie flying amongst them.

Just as they finished their conversation, Gareth stood up and clinked his spoon against his saucer to get the room's attention. Shyly, Amy rose to her feet beside him.

"Just a quick announcement, if I may," Gareth blushed a bright red as he began, "Amy and I wanted to let you know that we're expecting a baby in the summertime and Lewis is very excited to be a big brother!"

"Congratulations!" everyone said in unison, as Tanya and Betty exchanged knowing looks and the women all rushed to Amy's side to get all the details.

"It will be so lovely to have a new baby in the village," Jean cooed, "I'll start knitting straight away!"

"Aye, and you'll have all the babysitters you could ever wish for!" Betty added.

Unable to move with her ankle and boot to join the group, Flora waited until Amy was free to come over and then waved her across, "I'm so happy for you Amy!"

"Thank you, I'm just relieved to know why I've been feeling so out of sorts. Now, all we have to do is find somewhere to live together, I can't still be at my mam and dad's when I give birth!" Amy bit her lip in consternation, whereas Flora had a brilliant idea.

"Actually Amy, Billy's house is empty now, as you know, and it's all been cleared. It's only small, but you're welcome to rent it from the estate if you and Gareth would like to. Billy had been paying the same rent for about twenty years, I think, and I'd be happy to offer you the same terms."

"Really, Flora? Oh my goodness, thank you!" Amy

kissed Flora on the cheek and rushed over to talk to Gareth, who smiled across at Flora once he'd heard the news, giving her a big thumbs up.

"All okay, love?" Adam asked, coming over to join her.

"Yes, actually things might just be taking a turn for the better!" Flora said.

"I should hope so, they couldn't get much worse than the past week," Adam said, his tone serious, "I nearly lost you twice. I can't have that happen, not ever again."

And with that, Adam got down onto one knee, clasping Flora's hands in his in front of all their friends, and a hushed silence descended, "I know we haven't known each other for very long, not by some standards," Adam said, his shaking voice the sole indicator of his nerves, "but it took me only a short while to know that you're the one I've been waiting for."

"Aw, how lovely," Betty said in a stage whisper, clapping her hands in delight.

"Shh," Harry quieted her.

Adam smiled at the couple, "And I want us to grow old together and be like Betty and Harry when we're their age," he said, blushing, "sorry, this isn't how I planned it in my head…"

"No, go on," Flora encouraged, her eyes full of unshed tears.

"Flora Miller, it would do me the greatest honour if you would agree to be my wife. I love you, and I want to spend the rest of my life loving you and having you love me in return."

Flora opened her mouth to speak, at the very moment a small green bird landed on her shoulder and squawked, "You sexy beast!" causing everyone to laugh.

"Well," Tanya said, "answer the man!"

"Yes," Flora said, clearly for all to hear and without any doubt at all in her heart, "a thousand times yes!"

As Flora and Adam kissed, to the disgust of their feathered friend who hid his face under a wing, their friends clapped and cheered.

I love you," Flora whispered happily.

"And I love you," Adam replied in her ear, "and I can't wait to spend the rest of my life with you. A peaceful, quiet life, with no more murders on our doorstep!"

*Join Flora and Reggie in **"Out With the Old, In With the Choux"**, the next instalment in the Baker's Rise Mysteries series, to see whether a more peaceful life is, in fact, on the horizon!*

Out With the Old, In With the Choux

Baker's Rise Mysteries Book Five

Publication Date 22nd April 2022

Flora and Reggie are back in this fifth instalment of the Baker's Rise Mysteries series, with more shocks and surprises, and of course more of the community spirit and charm that make these books so popular!

Turning her attention to the manor house, Flora has some big decisions to make concerning what to do with The Rise.

In the meantime, however, the onset of spring encourages her to hire a new gardener to bring the grounds back to their former glory.

With a wedding to organise, and the bookshop and tearoom also keeping her busy, Flora feels pulled in too many directions. The last thing she needs is another murder investigation right on her doorstep!

Packed with twists and turns, colourful characters and more than a sprinkle of romance, this new mystery will certainly leave you hungry for more!

Fresh as a Daisy

The Lillymouth Mysteries Book One

Coming Summer 2022

Keep your eyes peeled for a brand new series coming to Amazon later this year!

Featuring a new lady vicar, a grumpy vicarage cat, and a seaside town in Yorkshire full of hidden secrets and more than a mystery or two!

ABOUT THE AUTHOR

Rachel Hutchins lives in northeast England with her husband, three children and their dog Boudicca. She loves writing both mysteries and romances, and enjoys reading these genres too! Her favourite place is walking along the local coastline, with a coffee and some cake!

You can connect with Rachel and sign up to her monthly **newsletter** via her website at: www.authorrachelhutchins.com

Alternatively, she has social media pages on:

Facebook: www.facebook.com/rahutchinsauthor

Instagram: www.instagram.com/ra_hutchins_author

Twitter: www.twitter.com/hutchinsauthor

OTHER BOOKS BY R. A. HUTCHINS

"The Angel and the Wolf"

What do a beautiful recluse, a well-trained husky, and a middle-aged biker have in common?
Find out in this poignant story of love and hope!

When Isaac meets the Angel and her Wolf, he's unsure whether he's in Hell or Heaven.
Worse still, he can't remember taking that final step.
They say that calm follows the storm, but will that be the case for Isaac?

Fate has led him to her door,
Will she have the courage to let him in?

"To Catch A Feather" (Found in Fife Book One)

When tragedy strikes an already vulnerable Kate Winters, she retreats into herself, broken and beaten. Existing rather than living, she makes a journey North to try to find herself, or maybe just looking for some sort of closure.

Cameron McAllister has known his own share of grief and love lost. His son, Josh, is now his only priority. In his forties and running a small coffee shop in a tiny Scottish fishing village, Cal knows he is unlikely to find love again.

When the two meet and sparks fly, can they overcome their past losses and move on towards a shared future, or are the memories which haunt them still too real?

These books, as well as others by Rachel, can be found on Amazon worldwide in e-book and paperback formats, as well as free to read on Kindle Unlimited.

Printed in Great Britain
by Amazon